ZOM-B ANGELS

DARREN SHAN

HarperCollins*PublishersLtd*

Zom-B Angels
Copyright © 2013 by Home of the Damned Limited
Illustrations © Warren Pleece
All rights reserved

Published by HarperCollins Publishers Ltd

First published in Great Britain in 2013
by Simon & Schuster UK Ltd
A CBS Company

First Canadian edition

HarperCollins books may be purchased for educational, business
or sales promotional use through our Special Markets Department.

HarperCollins Publishers Ltd
2 Bloor Street East, 20th Floor
Toronto, Ontario, Canada
M4W 1A8

www.harpercollins.ca

Library and Archives Canada Cataloguing in Publication
information is available upon request.

ISBN 978-1-44341-517-0

Printed and bound in the United States
RRD 9 8 7 6 5 4 3 2 1

OBE (Order of the Bloody Entrails) to
Phil Earle – gone, but only half forgotten!!

Edited with an angel's touch by:
Venetia Gosling
Kate Sullivan

Darren Shan is guided along the straight and narrow
by the Christopher Little Angels

THEN . . .

Becky Smith was at school the day the dead came back to life and took over the world. She tried to escape with a group of friends, but it wasn't meant to be. Her heart was torn from her chest and she became a zombie.

Several months later B recovered her senses in an underground military complex. The soldiers lumped her in with the zom heads, a pack of revitalised teenagers like her who had somehow regained their minds. They were told by their captors that they had to eat brains to stay conscious, and had a life expectancy of just a couple of years.

B would probably have remained a prisoner for the

rest of her days, if not for the intervention of a monstrous clown called Mr Dowling. He invaded with a team of mutants, set the zombies free and killed many of the staff. B didn't think he did it because he was pro-zombie — it looked to her like he did it for kicks.

Most of the zom heads were executed while trying to escape, but B made it out. She thought Rage might have got away as well. He was a self-serving bully who turned on his guards and proved just as clinical and merciless as they had been, casually killing one of the scientists before setting off on his own and warning his fellow zom heads not to follow him.

B roamed the streets of London for a while, mourning the loss of the normal world. It was a city of the dead, dotted with just a handful of living survivors. Some had chosen to stay, but others were trapped and desperately searching for a way out.

When B heard that the army was mounting a rescue operation, she went to offer herself to them, figuring they might be able to use her DNA to help other zombies recover their minds. But the soldiers saw her as a threat and tried to kill her. Once again the killer clown saved her. He slaughtered the humans, then asked her if she wanted to join him. B could think of nothing worse than teaming up with Mr Dowling, his creepy mutants and an eerie guy with owl-like eyes who had shown an interest in her even before the zombies attacked. She told him to stick his offer.

Wounded, bewildered and alone, B wandered across the river and staggered into an old building, County Hall, once the home of local government, now a deserted shell. At least that was what it looked like. But as B stared out of a window at the river, a man called to her by name and said he had been waiting for her.

NOW . . .

ONE

I whirl away from the window that overlooks the Thames. A man has entered the room through a door which I didn't notice on my way in. He's standing in the middle of the open doorway, arms crossed, smiling.

My survival instinct kicks in. With a roar, I hurl myself at the stranger, ignoring the flare of pain in my bruised, broken body. I curl my fingers into a fist and raise my hand over my head as I close on him.

The man doesn't react. He doesn't even uncross his arms. All he does is cock his head, to gaze with interest at my raised fist. His smile never slips.

I come to a stop less than a metre from the man, eyeing him beadily as my fist quivers above my head. If he'd tried to defend himself, I would have torn into him, figuring he was an enemy, as almost everybody else in this city seems to be. But he leaves himself open to attack and continues to smile.

'Who the hell are you?' I snap. He's dressed in a light grey suit, a white shirt and purple tie, and expensive-looking leather shoes. He has thin hair, neatly combed back, brown but streaked with grey. Calm brown eyes. Looks like he's in his forties.

'I am Dr Oystein,' he introduces himself.

'That supposed to mean something to me?' I grunt.

'I would be astonished if it did,' he says, then extends his right hand.

'You don't want to shake hands with me,' I sneer. 'Not unless you want to end up with a taste for brains.'

'I was an adventurous diner in my youth,' Dr Oystein says, his smile widening. 'I often boasted that I would eat the flesh or innards of just about any creature, except for humans. Alas, ironically, I can now eat nothing else.'

I frown and focus on his fingers. Bones don't stick out of them the way they poke out of every other zombie's, but now that I look closely, I see that the flesh at the tips is broken, a small white mound of filed-down bone at the centre of each pink whorl.

'Yes,' he says in answer to my unvoiced question. 'I am undead like you.'

I still don't take his hand. Instead I focus on his mouth. His teeth are nowhere near as jagged or as long as mine, but they're not the same as a normal person's either.

Dr Oystein laughs. 'You are wondering how I keep my teeth in such good shape, but there is no magic involved. I have been in this lifeless state a lot longer than you. One develops a knack for these things over time. I was brought up to believe that a gentleman should be neatly groomed and I have found myself as fastidious in death as I once was in life.

'Please take my hand, Becky. I will feel very foolish if you do not.'

'I don't give a monkey's how you feel,' I snort, and instead of shaking his hand, I listen closely for his heartbeat. When I don't detect one, I relax slightly.

'How do you know my name?' I growl. 'How could you have been expecting me? I didn't know that I was coming to County Hall. I wandered in randomly.'

Dr Oystein shakes his head. 'I have come to believe that nothing in life is truly random. In this instance it definitely was no coincidence that you wound up here. You were guided by the signs, as others were before you.'

I think back and recall a series of spray-painted, z-shaped symbols with arrows underneath. I've been following the arrows since I left the East End, sometimes because they happened to be pointing the way that I was travelling, but other times deliberately.

'Z for zombie,' Dr Oystein says as he sees my brain click. 'The signs mean nothing to reviveds, but what curious revitalised could turn a blind eye to such an intriguing mystery?'

'You know about reviveds and revitaliseds?'

'Of course.' He coughs lightly. 'In fact I was the one who coined the terms.'

'Who are you?' I whisper. '*What* are you?'

Dr Oystein sighs. 'I am a scientist and teacher. A

sinner and gentleman. A killer and would-be saviour. And, if you will do me the great honour, I would like to be your friend.'

The mysterious doctor waves his extended arm, once again inviting me to accept his hand. And this time, after a brief hesitation, even though I'm still suspicious, I lower my fist, uncurl my fingers and shake hands with the politely-spoken zombie.

TWO

'You have a strange accent,' I remark as Dr Oystein releases my hand. 'Where are you from?'

'Many places,' he says, slowly circling me, examining my wounds. 'My father was English but my mother was Norwegian. I was born in Norway and lived there for a while. Then my parents moved around Europe – my father had itchy feet – and I, of course, travelled with them.'

I try not to jitter as the doctor slips behind me. If he's been concealing a weapon, he'll be able to whip it out and strike. My shoulders tense as I imagine him driving a long knife between them. But he doesn't attack, just continues to circle, and soon he's facing me again.

'I heard that your heart had been ripped out,' he says. 'May I see?'

'How do you know that?' I scowl.

'I had contacts in the complex where you were previously incarcerated. I know much about you, but I hope to learn more. Please?' He nods towards my top.

With a sigh, I grab the hem of my T-shirt and lift it high, exposing my chest. Dr Oystein stares at the cavity on the left, where my heart once beat. Now there's just a jagged hole, rimmed by congealed blood and a light green moss.

'Fascinating,' the doctor murmurs. 'We zombies are all freaks of nature, each a walking medical marvel, but one tends to forget that. This is a reminder of our ability to defy established laws. You are a remarkable individual, Becky Smith, and you should be proud of the great wound which you bear.'

'Stop it,' I grunt. 'You'll make me blush.'

Dr Oystein sniffs. 'Not unless you are even more

remarkable than the rest of us. Without a heart, how would your body pump blood to your pale, pretty cheeks?'

Dr Oystein makes a gesture, inviting me to lower my T-shirt. As I do so, he steps across to the window where I was standing when he first addressed me. County Hall boasts one of the best views in the city. He looks out at the river, the London Eye, the Houses of Parliament and all the other deserted buildings.

'Such devastation,' he mumbles. 'You must have encountered horrors beyond your worst nightmares on your way to us. Am I correct?'

I think about all of the corpses and zombies I've seen ... Mr Dowling and the people he tormented and killed in Trafalgar Square ... his army of mutants and his bizarre sidekick, Owl Man ... the hunters who almost killed me ... Sister Clare of the Order of the Shnax, the way she transformed when I bit her ...

'You're not bloody wrong,' I wheeze.

'The world teeters on the brink,' Dr Oystein continues. 'It has been dealt a savage blow and I am sure that most of those who survived believe that there is no way back, regardless of what the puppets of the military might say in their radio broadcasts.'

'You've heard those too?'

'Oh yes. I tune in whenever I am in need of bitter-sweet amusement.' He looks back at me. 'There are many fools in this world, and it is no crime to be one of them. But to try and carry on as normal when all around you has descended into chaos . . . to try to convince others that you can restore order by operating as you did before . . . That goes beyond mere foolishness. That is madness and it will prove the true downfall of this world if we leave these people to their sad, petty, all too human devices.

'There *is* hope for civilisation as we once knew it. But if the living are to rise again, they will need our help, since only the conscious undead stand any sort of chance against the brain-hungry legions of the damned.'

Dr Oystein beckons me forward. I shuffle towards him slowly, not just because of the pain, but because I've almost been mesmerised by his words. He speaks like a hypnotist, slow, assured, serious.

When I join him at the window, Dr Oystein points to the London Eye, turning as smoothly and steadily as it did when thousands of tourists flocked there every day.

'I consider that a symbol of all that has been lost but which might one day be restored,' the doctor says. 'We keep it going, day and night, a beacon of living hope in this city of the dead. But no ordinary human could operate the Eye — they would be sniffed out and besieged by zombies. We, on the other hand, can. The dead will not bother us, since we are of no interest to them. That lack of interest is our strength and humanity's only hope of once again taking control of this planet.

'You are not the first revitalised to find your way here,' Dr Oystein goes on. 'There are others – weary, battered warriors – who have crawled through the streets of bloodshed and nightmares in search of sanctuary and hope, following the signs as you did.'

'Are you talking about zom heads?' I ask.

'Yes,' he says. 'But we do not use that term here. If you choose to stay with us and work for the forces of justice and mercy, you will come to think of yourself as we do, not as a zom head but an *Angel*.'

I snort. 'With wings and a harp? Pull the other one!'

'No wings,' Dr Oystein smiles. 'No harp either. But an Angel nonetheless.' He moves away from the window, towards the door. 'I have much to show you, Becky. You do not have to accompany me – you are free to leave any time that you wish, and always will be – but, if you are willing, I will take you on a tour and reveal some of the many secrets of the newly redefined County Hall.'

I stare at the open doorway. It's shadowy in the corridor outside. There could be soldiers waiting to jump me and stick me in a cell again.

'Why should I trust you?' I ask.

Dr Oystein shrugs. 'I could tell you to listen to your heart, but . . .'

The grisly joke eases my fears. Besides, there's no way I could turn back now. He's got me curious and, like a cat, I have to follow my nose and hope it doesn't lead me astray.

'All right, doc,' I grunt, limping over to him and

grinning, as if I haven't a care in the world. 'You can be my guide. Just don't expect a tip at the end.'

'I will ask for no tip,' he says softly. 'But I *will* ask for your soul.' He smiles warmly as I stiffen. 'There's no need to be afraid. When the time comes, I believe you will give it to me gladly.'

And with that cryptic remark, he leads me out of the room of light and into the vast, dark warren beyond.

THREE

'This is an amazing building,' Dr Oystein says as we wander through a series of long corridors, popping into massive, ornately decorated rooms along the way. 'Four thousand people worked here at its zenith. To think that it is now home to no more than a few dozen . . .' He makes a sighing sound.

'I came here a few times when I was younger,' I tell him. 'I went on the Eye, visited the aquarium and the London Dungeon, hung out in the arcade, ate at some of the restaurants. My dad brought us up one New Year's Eve for the fireworks. We queued for ages to get a drink from a shop nearby. Worth it though — it was a cool show.'

Dr Oystein pushes open a door to reveal a room with a handful of beds. They haven't been made up and I get the sense that nobody is using them.

'I had no idea how many revitaliseds would find their way to us,' he says. 'I hoped for many, feared for few, but we prepared for an influx to be on the safe side. There are many rooms like this, waiting for teenagers like you who will in all likelihood never come.'

I frown. 'Why just teenagers? Don't you accept adults too?'

'We would if any came, but adult revitaliseds are rare.'

'Why?' I ask.

'I will explain later,' he promises.

He closes the door and pushes on. After a while the style of the corridors and rooms changes and I realise we've crossed into one of the hotels which were part of County Hall before the zombie uprising.

'Oh, for the simple comforts of life,' Dr Oystein says

drily as we check out a suite that's bigger than my family's old flat in the East End. 'Did you ever stay in a hotel like this, Becky?'

'No. And it's B,' I tell him. 'That's what everybody calls me.'

'Is that what you prefer?'

'Yeah.'

He nods. 'As you wish. We all have the right to choose our own name.'

'How about you?' I counter. 'Dr Oystein's a mouthful. What's your first name?'

He smiles. 'Oystein *is* my first name. It has been so long since I used my surname that I have almost forgotten what it is.'

We double back on ourselves, but take a different route. This place is a maze. My head is spinning as I try to chart all the twists and turns, in case I need to make a quick getaway. The doctor seems like a nice old bloke, but I'm taking nothing for granted.

'How many rooms are there?' I ask.

'Far too many to count,' Dr Oystein says. 'We use very few of them. It's a pity we cannot make more use of the space, but we do not have the numbers at the moment. Maybe one day we can bring it fully back to life, but for the time being we must rattle around in it.'

'Why don't you move somewhere smaller?'

Dr Oystein coughs as if embarrassed. 'To be honest, I always had a fondness for County Hall. When I was casting around for a base, this was my first choice. The Angels seem to share my love for the building. I hope that it will come to feel like home for you over time, as it has for us.'

'So who lives here with you?' I ask. 'You haven't told me about the set-up yet, how you came to be here, who your Angels are, how you plan to save the world.'

'Those questions will all be answered,' he assures me. 'We do not keep secrets from one another. We are open in all that we do. But there is no need to rush. As you adjust and settle in, we will reveal more of our work and background to you, until you know as much about us as I do.'

I don't like being told to wait, but this is his gig. Besides, I'm exhausted and my brain hurts, so I don't think I could take in much more anyway. There's one thing that does disturb me though, and I want to bring it up before pushing on any further.

'How come there are no regular zombies here? Every other big, dark building that I've seen has been packed with them.'

'I had already recruited a small team of Angels before I established a permanent base,' he says. 'We drove out the reviveds before we moved in.'

'That must have been messy.'

'It was actually the easiest thing in the world,' he replies. 'With their sharp sense of hearing, reviveds – like revitaliseds – are vulnerable to high-pitched noises. So we simply installed a few speakers and played a string of high notes through them, which proved unbearable for those who had taken up residence. They moved out without any protest, then we slid in after them and shored up the entrances.'

'I got in without any hassle,' I remind him.

'We saw you coming on our security cameras,' he says. 'We switched off the speakers – we repositioned them around the building once we had moved in, and normally play the noises on a constant loop, to keep stray reviveds at bay – and made sure a door was open when you arrived.'

We come to a huge room and I catch my first glimpse of what I assume are some of Dr Oystein's Angels. There's a small group of them at the centre of the room, in a boxing ring, sparring. They're my sort of age, no more than a year or two older or younger than me.

'They spend most of their days training,' Dr Oystein says.

'For what?'

'War.'

I swivel to look at him, but he doesn't return my gaze.

'The years ahead will be hard,' he says quietly. 'We will be tested severely, and I am sure at times we will be found wanting. We face many battles, some of which we are certain to lose. But if we prepare as best we can, and have faith in ourselves and the justness of our cause, we will triumph in the end.'

I snort. 'I hate to burst your bubble, doc, but if those Angels are like me, you'd better tell them to get their

arses in gear. In another year or two we'll be pushing up daisies. You can't win a war if all your troops are rotting in the grave.'

Dr Oystein frowns. 'What are you talking about?'

'Our limited lifespan. We've only got a year and a half, two years max. Then our senses will dissolve, our brains will melt and we'll be dead meat. If you've got a war you want to win, you'd better crack on and –'

'You were told many things when you were a prisoner,' Dr Oystein interrupts. 'Some were true. Some, you must surely know, were not. Your captors wanted to bend you to their will. They told you lies to dampen your spirit, to break it, to make you theirs.'

I stare at him, hardly daring to believe what he's telling me. 'You mean it was bullshit about me only having a year or two to live?'

'Of the highest grade,' he smiles.

'I'm not going to die soon?' I cry.

'You are already dead,' he says.

'You know what I mean,' I groan. 'My brain's not going to pop and leave me truly dead?'

'Far from it.'

30

I clench my fingers tight and give the air a victory punch. 'Bloody *YES*, mate! You've made my day, doc. I was ready to accept an early end, but as crap as my excuse for a life is, I'd rather this than no life at all.'

'Most of us share your view,' he chuckles, then grows serious. 'But they did not tell you a total lie. We do not age the same way that humans do. Our lifespan, for want of a better term, is not what an average human might expect.'

'So it was half true,' I growl. 'Those are the best sort of lies, I guess. Go on then, doc, hit me with the bad news. I can take it. How long do I have? Twenty years? Ten? Five?'

'We cannot be absolutely certain,' he says. 'I have run many tests and made a series of predictions. But we have no long-term data to analyse, and will not have for many decades to come. There are all sorts of genetic kinks of which I might be ignorant.'

'Your guess is better than mine,' I smile. 'I won't blame you if you're off by a few years.'

'Very well. I won't tease you with a dramatic build-up. As I said, this is a rough estimate, but based on the

FOUR

I'm in shock for ages. To go from thinking you have only months to live, to being told you might be hanging around for a couple of millennia ... it's a cataclysmic leap and my mind whirls as we continue the tour.

We visit a kitchen where a good-looking, stylishly dressed woman with a big smile is scraping brains from inside severed human heads and dumping them in a mixing bowl. Dr Oystein introduces us, but I forget the woman's name even before we leave the room.

'Some of the heads are delivered to us from people who die of natural causes in human compounds,' he

says. 'We have contacts among the living who view us as allies, and they give us what they can. But most come from fresh corpses that we found in morgues or dug up not long after the first zombie attacks. I knew brains would be a pressing issue, so I made them my number-one priority. For a couple of weeks, grave-robbing was practically our full-time occupation.'

He tells me how he's trying to create a synthetic sub-stitute that will give us the nutrients we need, so that we don't have to rely on reaping brains from dead humans in future, but I'm barely listening.

More bedrooms, another training centre – again, I only spot teenagers – and the impressive council cham-ber. Dr Oystein starts waffling on about the history of County Hall, but I can't focus. I keep thinking about the centuries stretching out ahead of me, the incredibly long life that has been dropped on me without any warning.

Halfway down another of the building's long corri-dors, I stop and shake my head. 'This is crazy,' I shout. 'You're telling me I'm gonna live at least twenty times longer than any human?'

'Yes,' Dr Oystein says calmly.

'How the hell can anyone last that long?'

He shrugs. 'A living person could not. But we are dead. We do not age as we used to. If we take care of our bodies, and sustain ourselves by eating brains, we can defy the laws of living flesh.'

'Then what's to say we won't live forever?' I challenge him. 'Where did you pull two or three thousand years from? If we don't age –'

'We *do* age,' he cuts in smoothly. 'I said that we do not age as we used to, but we definitely age, only at a much slower rate. Our external appearance will not change much, except for scarring, wrinkling and dis-colouring. Our internal organs are to all intents and purposes irrelevant, so even if they crumble away, it won't really matter.

'Only our brains are susceptible to the ravages of time. From what my tests have revealed, they are slowly deteriorating. If they continue to fail at the rate I have noted in the subjects that I have been able to assess, we should manage to hold ourselves together for two or three thousand years. But it could be less, it could be more. Only time will tell.'

I shake my head again, still struggling to come to terms with the revelation.

'Try not to think about it too much,' Dr Oystein says kindly. 'I know it is a terrifying prospect — a long life seems enviable until one is presented with the reality of it and has to think of all those days and nights to come, how hard it will be to fill them, to keep oneself amused for thousands of years. And it is even harder since we do not sleep and thus have more time to deal with than the living.

'But as with everything in life, you will learn to cope. I'm not saying it will be easy or that you won't have moments of doubt, but I suggest you turn a blind eye to your longevity for now. You can brood about it later.' He sighs. 'There will be plenty of time for brooding.'

'Why tell me about it at all if that's the case?' I snap.

Dr Oystein shrugs. 'It is important that you know. It is one of the first things that I tell my Angels. Our approach to life – or our semblance of it – differs greatly depending on how much time we have to play with.'

'Come again?' I frown.

'If you think you have only a year to live, you might

behave recklessly, risking life and limb, figuring you have little to lose. Most people treat their bodies with respect when they realise that they may need them for longer.'

'I suppose,' I grumble.

Dr Oystein smiles. 'You will see the brighter side of your circumstances once you recover from the shock. But if it still troubles you, at least you have the comfort of knowing that you will not have to go through this alone. We are all in the same boat. We will support one another over the long decades to come.'

'All right,' I mutter and we start walking again. My mind's still whirling, but I try to put thoughts of my long future on hold and focus on the tour again. It's hard – I have a sick feeling in my stomach, like I get if I go too long without eating brains – but the doctor's right. I can obsess about this later. If I try to deal with it now, I'll go mad thinking about it. And madness is the last thing I want to face in my state. I mean, who fancies spending a couple of thousand years as a slack-jawed, drooling nutter!

FIVE

The tour draws to its conclusion shortly after our conversation in the corridor. We pass through one of the large courtyards of County Hall – I remember seeing them from up high when I went on the Eye in the past – and into a room which has been converted into a lab, lots of test tubes and vials, some odd-looking machines beeping away quietly in various places, pickled brains and other internal organs that have been set up for dissection and examination.

'This is not my main place of work,' Dr Oystein says. 'I maintain another laboratory elsewhere in the city. I had a string of similar establishments in different countries around the world, but I do not know what has become of them since the downfall.'

He looks at me seriously. 'I told you that we keep no secrets from one another here, and that is the truth, with one key exception. The other laboratory is where I conduct the majority of my experiments and tests, and where I keep the records of all that I have discovered over the years.'

'You mean you haven't just started researching zombies since the attacks?'

'No. I am over a hundred years old and have been studying the undead since the mid-1940s.' As I gawp at him, he continues as if what he's told me is no big deal. 'I have a team of scientists who have been working with me for many years. They are based at my main research centre. I lost a lot of good men and women when the city fell, but enough survived to assist me in my efforts going forward.

'I dare not reveal the location of that laboratory to anyone. It is not an issue of trust but of fear. There are dark forces stacked against us. You are aware of the one who calls himself Mr Dowling?'

'You know about the clown?' I gasp.

Dr Oystein nods sombrely. 'I will tell you more about him later. For now, know only that he is our enemy, the most dangerous foe we will ever face. He yearns for the complete destruction of mankind. I guard the secrets of deadly formulas that Mr Dowling could use to wipe out the living. If I told you where my laboratory was, and if he captured you and forced the information from you ...'

I smile shakily. 'That's all right, doc. I know what a bastard he is. You don't need to feel bad about not sharing.'

'Yet I do,' he mutters glumly, then grimaces. 'Well, as limited as this laboratory is, it does feature one of my more refreshing inventions, a device which is literally going to blow your mind. Come and see.'

Dr Oystein quickens his pace and leads me to four tall, glass-fronted cylinders near the rear of the lab. Each is about three metres high and one metre in diameter. One is filled with a dark grey liquid that looks like thick, gloopy soup.

'I have a complicated technical name for these,' Dr

Oystein says. 'But one of my American Angels nick-named them Groove Tubes some years ago and it stuck.'

'What are they for?' I ask.

'Recovery and recuperation.' The doctor pokes one of the deep gashes on my left arm and I wince. 'As you will have noticed, our bodies do not generate new cells to repair cuts and other wounds. Our only natural defence mechanism is the green moss which sprouts on open gashes. The moss prevents significant blood loss and holds strands of shredded flesh together, but it is not a curative aid. Broken bones don't mend. Cuts never properly close. Pain, once inflicted, must be endured indefinitely.'

'Tell me about it,' I huff, having been hunched over and limping since Trafalgar Square.

'We can endure the pain when we have to,' Dr Oystein continues, 'but it is a barrier. It is hard to focus when you are wracked with agony. Like you, I have suf-fered much in my time. I realised long ago that I needed to find some way to combat the pain, to ensure it did not distract me from my work. I conducted many experiments and eventually came up with the Groove Tube. In the fledgling world of zombie chemistry, this probably ranks as the most significant invention to date. If the undead awarded Nobel prizes . . .'

He smiles at the absurdity of the suggestion, then clears his throat. 'Although the technology is complicated, the results are easy to explain. The liquid inside a Groove Tube is a specially formulated solution which uses modified brain cells as its core ingredient. If you are undead and you immerse yourself, the solution stimulates some of the healing functions of your body.

'Your lesser wounds will heal inside the Tube. The cuts on your elbows and head will scab over, as they would have when you were alive. It won't have much of a visible effect on the hole in your chest, but it will patch up the worst damage and you will not bleed so freely.

'There are other benefits. Broken bones will mesh. Your eyesight will improve and your eyes will sting less. You will not need to use drops so often. You might get a few of your taste buds back, but that sensation won't last for long. You will come out feeling energetic and the pain will be far less than it currently is.'

'Sounds like a miracle cure,' I mutter, suspicious, as I always am, of anything that sounds too good to be true.

'A miracle, perhaps,' he says, 'but not a full-blown cure. The effects are not permanent. If a bone has broken, the gel holding the two parts together will start to fail after a few years. All wounds will reopen in time. But you can immerse yourself again when that happens and be healed afresh. It is too soon to know if we can use the Tubes indefinitely, but so far I have not noticed any limit on the number of times that they can work their wonders on a given body.'

'Fair enough, doc. You've sold me.' I start to strip.

'One moment,' he stops me. 'I want you to be fully aware of what you are letting yourself in for.'

'I knew it,' I scowl. 'What's the catch?'

'We cannot sleep,' Dr Oystein says. 'Wakefulness is a curse of the undead and I have been unable to find a cure for it. But when we enter a Groove Tube, we hallucinate.'

'Go on,' I growl.

'It is like getting high,' the doctor murmurs, staring longingly at the grey gloop inside the cylinder. 'As the solution fills your lungs – you cannot drown, so it will not harm you, although we'll have to pump you dry when we pull you out – you will start to experience a sense of deep, overwhelming bliss. You will have visions and your brain will tune out the world beyond the Tube, as you enter a dreamlike state.'

'Sounds good to me,' I beam.

'It *is* good,' he nods. 'But there are dangers which you should be aware of. One is the addictive nature of the experience. You will not want to leave. I could let my Angels soak in the Tubes regularly, but I do not. They are reserved for the treatment of serious wounds. The main reason I insist on that is to help them avoid becoming addicted. You may wish to re-enter the Tube at the end of the process, but I will not permit it. They are for medicinal – not recreational – purposes only.'

'Understood. And the real kicker?'

Dr Oystein nods. 'You are sharper than most of my Angels, B. Yes, I have held back the real kicker, as you call it, until the end.' He pauses. 'It will take two or three weeks for your wounds to fully heal. During that time you will be unaware of all that is happening around you. It would be a simple thing for me or anyone else to attack you while you are in that suspended state. You will have no way of defending yourself. If someone wanted to cut your head open and pulp your brain, it would be child's play. Or we could just leave you inside the Tube and never pull you out — if we did not haul you clear, you would bob up and down inside the solution for the rest of your existence, never fully waking. Once you succumb to the allure of the Groove Tube, you will be at our mercy.'

I stare at the doctor long and hard. 'That's a pretty big ask, doc.'

'Yes,' he says.

'Can I wait to make my decision?'

'Of course.'

'Will anything bad happen to me if I choose not to enter the Tube?' I watch him warily for his answer, ready to bolt for freedom if I get the feeling that he's spinning me a lie.

'If you mean will your wounds worsen, no. You will have to endure the pain, but that is all.'

I nod slowly, thinking it over. Then I decide to hell with it. Maybe I'm a fool, but I want to trust this guy. I *need* to trust him. I've felt so alone since I came back from the dead, even when I've been surrounded by others. Without someone to believe in, what's the point of going on?

'All right, doc,' I sigh as I take off the rest of my clothes. 'I can't be bothered waiting. I'm hopping in. You might have to adjust the temperature for me though — I like my bathwater *hot*.'

SIX

GgggggggggROOOOOOOOveeeeeeeeee!!!!!!!

SEVEN

Next thing I know, I'm flopping about on the floor of the lab like a dying fish, vomiting up liquid. The room seems extraordinarily bright. I moan and start to shield my eyes with a hand. Before I can, someone tosses a towel over my head and says something. I can't hear them clearly, so I slide my hand in under the towel to stick a finger in my ear and clear it out.

'No!' comes a roar loud enough to penetrate even my clogged ear canals. 'You might damage your ear with the bone sticking out of your finger.'

I'd forgotten about the bones. Lowering the hand, I

try to ask the person their name, but my throat and mouth are full of the solution from the Tube.

'Keep as still as you can,' a boy says. 'We know what we're doing.'

Someone lifts the towel and gently runs a cotton bud round the inside of my left ear, then my right. A plastic tube slides up under my chin and I'm instructed to feed it down my throat.

'I know it's gross,' a girl says, 'but we have to pump your stomach dry, otherwise you won't be able to talk.'

With a grimace, I stick the tube into my mouth – it's tricky because my teeth sprouted while I was blissed out – and force it down. When it can't play out any more, I hold it in place while a machine is switched on, and keep my lips open wide while liquid is pumped out of my stomach.

After several minutes there's nothing left to come up. The machine is turned off and I'm handed a pair of sunglasses.

'Put them on,' the girl tells me. 'The room will still seem brighter than normal, but you'll soon adjust.'

I slip on the shades and tug the towel from my head.

Squinting against the light, I spot the boy and girl, both a bit younger than me.

'*Groo gar goo?*' I gurgle.

'Take it easy,' the boy says, picking up a smaller hooked tube. 'Your lungs are still full. We have to slide this down into them. Are you ready?'

'*Ghursh.*'

'I'll take that as a yes,' he smirks and carefully slides the tube into my mouth. He has a torch attached to a headband, the sort that surgeons use, and he shines it between my teeth as he searches for the correct opening. When he finds it, he begins to poke the tube down my windpipe. It's a horrible feeling and my instinct is to grind my teeth together and snap through the tube. But I know these guys are trying to help, so I fight the urges of my body.

The boy switches on the machine again and pumps my lungs dry. When he turns it off and withdraws the tube, I cough and scowl at the pair.

'Ish that iht?' I mumble, words still coming out garbled because of my oversized teeth, but a lot clearer than before.

'Just about,' the girl giggles. 'But the pump doesn't force out every last drop. The liquid will have made its way through your digestive system. We need to give you an enema.'

'What'sh that?' I ask.

She holds up a third tube. 'We need to insert this up your . . .' She nods at my bum.

'Ihf you try to shtick that fhing ihn me, I'll ram iht up *your* hole!' I bark, slapping the tube from her hands.

'Fine,' she shrugs. 'You can wear a nappy for the next week instead.'

I swear and glare at the grinning pair. 'Mahke him turn his bahck,' I growl.

'Like it's something I *want* to see,' the boy snorts and turns away, focusing his attention elsewhere.

I've never had an enema before, and I don't ever want one again, and that's all I'm saying about that!

When the girl has cleared me out, she leads me to a shower and I hose myself down, washing off the grey gunk from the Groove Tube. When I step out, she hands me a robe. I pull it on gratefully. Even though I'm cleaner than I've ever been, I feel strangely soiled.

'No need to be ashamed,' the girl says as I towel my hair dry. 'We all have to suffer this when we come out of the Groove Tubes. It's a small price to pay. Look at your arms.'

I roll up the sleeves of the robe and study my elbows. When I slid into the Tube, the flesh around them had been ripped to pieces, the bone exposed in places. Now they look almost as good as new. Scarred, pink flesh, but whole and healthy-looking.

I part the front of my robe and examine the hole in the left side of my chest. It's still an ugly, gaping wound, but it doesn't look as messy as it did. Some of the green moss has come away in the tank, and it's not as foresty as it was.

I close my robe again and stare at the glass-fronted cylinder. The liquid is being drained from it, but slowly. It's murkier than before, having absorbed dead cells, blood and all sorts of gunk from my body while I was bobbing up and down inside. I showered thoroughly before getting in, however many weeks ago it was, but there was still a lot of dirt to come out.

'Where'sh Docktohr Oyshteeen?' I ask.

'He's not here,' the boy says. 'He's been gone the last week or more, at his other laboratory. He told us to apologise on his behalf. He would have liked to be here to welcome you back into the world, but his work called him away.'

'It often does,' the girl says, 'so don't take it personally.'

'I whon't. Who are yhou?'

'I'm Cian,' the boy says.

'And I'm Awnya,' the girl adds. 'We're twins.'

'The only twin revitaliseds in London as far as we know,' Cian says proudly.

'Probably the world,' Awnya beams.

'Congrachulayshuns,' I mutter sarcastically.

'We're in charge of clothing, bedding, furniture and so on,' Cian tells me. 'If there's anything you need that you can't be bothered going to look for yourself, let us know and we'll do our best to get it for you, whether it's designer clothes, a certain brand of shoe or a specific type of hat.'

'We got rid of your old clothes,' Awnya says, 'but we held on to the slouch hat in case it had sentimental value. You'll find it on a shelf in your bedroom.'

'Thanksh.'

My gaze returns to the Groove Tube, longingly this time. I don't remember much after Dr Oystein helped me climb inside. I recall the feeling of the liquid oozing down my throat – surprisingly not as unpleasant as when I had to force it back up – but then I drifted off into a blissful state where everything seemed warm and right. It was like I used to feel when I'd lie in bed on a Sunday morning, having stayed up late to watch horror movies the night before, not asleep but not yet fully awake. The feeling of being somewhere comfortable and safe, the world not totally real, still part dreamy.

I smoked a bit of weed back in the day – Mum would have killed me if she'd known! – but I didn't try anything more exotic. Based on what friends of mine who had done harder drugs told me, the feeling I had inside the Groove Tube must have been a lot like going on a headtrip. Part of me wants to crawl back inside and bliss out again, return to the land of dreams and stay there forever, escape this world of the living dead. But I recall what Dr Oystein told me about only using the Tubes to cure injuries. Besides, that would be like committing suicide. This is a bad, mad world, but running away from it isn't the answer. Well, it's not *my* answer.

I'm about to ask the twins to show me to my room when I glance at the other Groove Tubes and come to a halt. One of the Tubes is occupied by a large teenager. He has a big head, hair cut close, small ears, beady eyes. Fat, rosy cheeks, a chunk bitten out of the left one. He looks like a real bruiser, and I know that in this case looks are definitely *not* deceptive.

The last time I saw this guy was in a corridor deep underground. He'd just killed a scientist and scooped the still-warm brain from the dead man's skull. He was a zom head like me and the others, but he took off solo, leaving the rest of us to rot. He cared only for himself and was prepared to kill his guardians and betray his friends as long as it suited his own selfish purposes.

He looks comical, floating in the Tube, naked, eyes open as they are on all zombies, but expression distant. He's unaware of everything, defenceless, at the mercy of Dr Oystein and his Angels.

And me.

But I'm not prepared to show him mercy, just as he didn't show any to me, Mark or the other zom heads. This bastard deserves execution more than most, and I'm just the girl to do the world that small favour.

'*Rhage!*' I snarl, pressing my face up close to the glass of the Groove Tube. Then I step back and look around eagerly for a weapon to kill him.

EIGHT

'No, B,' Cian snaps and tries to pull me back.

I wrestle with the boy and throw him to the floor. Awnya rushes me, but I grab her by the throat, then slam her to the ground beside her brother. Good to see the old fighting touch hasn't deserted me.

The twins quickly and easily dealt with, I turn back towards the Groove Tube, fingers flexing, snarling viciously. But before I can focus, someone says, 'Take one more step towards him and I'll fry you.'

I pause and peer around the lab. At first I can't see anyone. Then he moves and I spot him, standing close to the door which opens on to the courtyard. He takes several strides towards me and his face swims into view. A burly man with brown hair and stubble, wearing a dark blue outfit that wouldn't look out of place on a security guard. The last time I saw him, he was in military fatigues.

'*Rheilly?*' I gawp.

The soldier smiles tightly. 'None other.'

'What the hell are yhou doing here?'

'The same as usual — guarding those who don't deserve guarding.'

Reilly stops a couple of metres from me. He's holding some sort of a gun, but it doesn't look like any I've seen before.

'Step away from the Tube, B.'

'Shkroo yhou, arsh hohl,' I snap.

His smile broadens. 'That was one of the first things you said when we originally filed your teeth down, back when you revitalised. It's like we've come full circle. I feel nostalgic.'

'Fhunny guy,' I sneer, than tap the glass of the Groove Tube. 'He killed Docktohr Sherverus.'

'I know.'

'Pohked his eye out, cut his head open and tuhcked in.'

'I'm not a goldfish,' Reilly sniffs. 'I was there. I remember.'

'Sho I'm gonna kill him. Retchribooshun.'

'Don't make me laugh,' Reilly snorts. 'You hated Dr Cerveris. His death didn't matter to you in the slightest.'

I shake my head. 'Yesh, I hated him. But I didn't whant to kill him. Rhage ish a shavage. Becaush ohf him, Mark and the othersh are dead.'

'I know,' Reilly says, softly this time. 'That sucks, the way they slaughtered the revitaliseds. It's one of the reasons I cut my ties with Josh and the rest after they'd regained control of the complex. But Dr Oystein offered Rage a home when he came here, wounded like you were, in need of sanctuary, even though he wouldn't admit it. Rage was dubious, especially when he saw you. He wanted to kill you, like you want to kill him. But Dr Oystein protected you and promised to do the same for Rage while he was incapable of defending himself.'

'Don't care,' I growl. 'Gonna kill him anywhay.'

Reilly raises his gun.

'Don't tell me it'sh me ohr him,' I groan.

'No,' Reilly says. 'I'm not going to kill you. This is a stun gun. It fires spiked electrodes into your flesh, then fries you with a burst of electricity that would bring down an elephant. You're tough, B, but this will floor you for at least half an hour. Trust me, you do *not* want to put yourself through that. However bad your enema felt, it's nothing in comparison with this.'

'Yhou were whatching that?' I snarl.

'Don't worry,' he grins. 'I averted my gaze during the more sensitive moments. I've visited the great pyramids, Petra, the temples of Angkor Wat. Your bunghole doesn't rank high on my list of must-sees.'

I laugh despite myself. 'Yhou're a bashtard, Rheilly.'

'Takes one to know one,' he retorts. 'Now step away from the Tube and let the twins escort you to your quarters.'

'What ihf I shay shkroo the quahrters? What ihf I don't whant anything to do with idiotsh who give shelter to a monshter like him?'

Reilly shrugs. 'You need the Angels a lot more than they need you. Dr Oystein will be sad if you reject his offer of hospitality, but as for the rest of us, nobody will miss you.'

I come close to leaving. I'm on the verge of telling Reilly that he can marry Rage if he loves him that much. Then Awnya steps up beside me and shakes her head.

'Don't do it, B. It's horrible out there. Cian and I were lucky — we had each other. But we were lonely until we came here. And scared.'

'We saw terrible things,' Cian murmurs. 'We *did* terrible things.' He pulls his jumper aside to reveal a deep, moss-encrusted bite mark on his shoulder. 'We became monsters when we turned. Dr Oystein doesn't care. He gave us a home, and he'll give you one too if you let him.'

'But thish guy ish a bruhte!' I yell. 'He'sh not like ush. He killed when he didn't need to and kept the brain for himshelf.'

'Are you pissed because he didn't share Dr Cerveris's brain with you?' Reilly chuckles.

66

'No,' I sneer. 'I'm pisshed becaush Mark was killed. Ihf Rhage had let the resht of ush eat, the othersh wouldn't have needed to kill Mark. Maybe Josh would have shpared them too.'

'I doubt it,' Reilly says. 'I wasn't privy to the decisions that were made that day, but I think all of the zom heads were scheduled for execution once it became clear that we had to evacuate. They didn't dare let you guys run wild. I don't know why Josh let you go, but the others would have been eliminated no matter what.'

'Maybe,' I concede. 'That doeshn't change the fact that Rhage did whrong.'

'No,' Reilly agrees. 'It doesn't. But it's part of my job now to look after those who need help, regardless of anything they did or didn't do in the past. I might not like it – in fact forget about *might*, I *don't* – but we're playing by Dr Oystein's rules here. Maybe he sees potential for good in Rage that you or I missed. Or maybe he's taking a gamble and will come to view him as the sly, turncoat killer that we both know and loathe. If he does, and he asks me to handle the situation, I'll be only too delighted to pay back Rage for what he did to Cerveris and the others, but –'

'Othersh?' I interrupt.

'Cerveris wasn't the only one he killed while he was breaking out,' Reilly says. 'I didn't have many friends in that place, but he murdered a couple of guys I knew who were good men, just trying to do their job. I've no sympathy for him.'

'Then why don't you help me shettle the shcore?' I whine.

'Because I trust Dr Oystein,' Reilly says simply. 'I trust his judgement even more than my own. I've only known him for a month and a bit, so maybe that's a crazy claim, but it's how I feel. I went along with orders underground because that was what I'd always done. Everything had gone to hell and I thought the only way to deal with the madness was to carry on as if it was business as usual.

'But I'm cooperating with Dr Oystein because I truly believe that he can lead the living out of this mess, that he can help those of us who survived to find a better way forward. If he says that Rage has the same rights as the rest of the revitaliseds, who am I to question him?'

I swear bitterly, knowing I can't win this argument. My choice is clear — walk away and return to the chaos and loneliness of the undead city beyond these walls, or play along and see what Dr Oystein has to say for himself when he returns.

'Thish ishn't ohver,' I tell Reilly. 'Rhage and I have unfhinished bishness.'

'Sure you do,' Reilly laughs. 'Just don't try to sort it out while I'm guarding him — if we got into a fight and you scratched me, you'd turn me into a revived, and I don't think either of us wants that, do we?'

'Don't be sho shure about that,' I jeer, showing him my fangs, but it's an idle threat. I'd hate to have his blood on my hands.

I give Reilly a long, slow stare. Then Cian and Awnya drag me out of the lab. I leave reluctantly, finding it hard to tear my gaze away from Reilly and the devious, deceitful creep bobbing up and down inside the grey, clammy solution of the Groove Tube.

NINE

I scowl and mutter to myself as I stomp through the courtyard. Cian and Awnya have to jog to keep up.

'You really like that guy then?' Cian jokes.

'He abahndhoned me and my fhriends,' I growl. 'Lehft ush to be killed. Called ush a bunch of looshers. He'sh shkum.'

'Dr Oystein will be able to help him,' Awnya says confidently.

'He doeshn't need help,' I sneer. 'He needsh execy-ooshun.'

I shake my head, sigh and slow down. We're still in

the courtyard. I look up at the sky. It's a cloudy, grey day, I'm guessing late morning or early afternoon.

'Here,' Cian says, handing me a small metal file. I think it's one of the ones I was carrying when I arrived. 'I was going to give you this in your room, but maybe you'd prefer it now.'

'Thanksh.' I set to work on my teeth – it's tricky without a mirror – and grind away at those which have sprouted the most. The twins wait patiently, saying nothing as bits of enamel go flying across the yard. When I feel halfway normal, I lower the file, run my tongue around my teeth and say my name and old address out loud. I'm still not perfect, but a lot better than I was before.

'How long was I in the Groove Tube?' I ask.

'Just over three weeks,' Awnya says.

'Twenty-four days,' Cian elaborates.

'*Twenty-four Days Later*,' I say sombrely, deepening my voice to sound like a movie announcer. The twins stare at me blankly. 'You know, like *Twenty-eight Days Later*?' They haven't a clue what I'm talking about. 'Didn't you watch zombie movies before all this happened?'

72

'No,' Awnya says. 'They scared me.'

'And we always watched movies together,' Cian says. 'So if one of us didn't like a certain type of film, the other couldn't watch it either.'

'That's why I never got to see any chick flicks,' Awnya says, shooting her twin a dark look.

'Life's too short,' Cian snorts. 'Even if we live to be three thousand, it will still be too short as far as chick flicks are concerned.'

'Well, I won't let you watch any zombie movies either,' Awnya pouts.

'Like I want to watch any now,' Cian laughs.

I study the twins. They're about the same height. Both have blond hair and fair skin. They look similar and are dressed in matching, cream-coloured clothes. A chunk has been bitten out of Awnya's left hand, just above her little finger. I see bone shining through the green, wispy moss. In the daylight they look even younger than they did in the lab, no more than twelve or thirteen.

'Were you guys attacked at the same time?' I ask.

'Yeah,' Cian says.

'But I got bitten first,' Awnya says. 'He could have escaped but he came back for me. The idiot.'

'I wouldn't have bothered if I'd known you were going to tuck into me,' Cian sniffs, rubbing his shoulder through the fabric of his jumper.

'She turned on you?' I smirk wickedly.

'It wasn't her fault,' Cian says, quick to defend his sister. 'She didn't know what she was doing. None of us did when we were in that state. At least she didn't rip my skull open, or that would have been the real end of me.'

'Your nasty brain would have turned my stomach,' Awnya says and the twins beam at each other.

'Nice to see you don't bear a grudge,' I note.

Cian shrugs. 'What's done is done. Besides, this way we can carry on together. I wouldn't have wanted to escape and live normally if it meant leaving Awnya behind. I'd rather be a zombie with her than a human on my own.'

'Pass me the sick bag,' I groan, but grin to let them know I'm only joking.

It starts to rain, so we step inside and the twins lead me to my bedroom.

'How long have you guys been here?' I ask.

'Ages,' Awnya yawns. 'We revitalised quickly, less than a week after we were turned.'

'We were among the first to recover their senses,' Cian boasts. 'Dr Oystein says we're two of his most incredible Angels.'

I frown. 'This place was open for business that soon after the attacks?'

'No,' Awnya says. 'We wandered for a couple of weeks before we noticed the arrows.'

'That was a scary time,' Cian says softly and the pair link hands.

'Dr Oystein was based in Hyde Park when we found him,' Awnya continues. 'He put up a tent in the middle of the park and that's where his first Angels joined him and sheltered. He was already working on modifying this place, but it was another few weeks before we were able to move in.'

'Did he have Groove Tubes in Hyde Park?'

'He had one,' Cian says, 'but it was no good. There was a generator to power it, but the noise attracted reviveds. They kept attacking and knocking it out —

they didn't like the sound. He wasn't able to mount a proper guard, so in the end he left it until we moved here.'

'A couple of revitaliseds died because of that,' Awnya says sadly. 'They were so badly wounded, in so much pain, that they killed themselves.'

'I've never seen Dr Oystein look so miserable,' Cian croaks. 'If he could cry, I think he'd still be weeping now.'

There's a long silence, broken only by the sound of our footsteps.

'How did you end up doing this?' I ask. 'Taking people round and getting stuff for them?'

'We're good at it,' Awnya smiles. 'Dr Oystein says we're like jackdaws — we can find a pearl anywhere.'

'Our mum was a shopaholic,' Cian says. 'She dragged us everywhere with her. We got to be pretty good at finding our way round stores and tracking down items that she was interested in. When Dr Oystein saw how quickly we could secure materials, he put us in charge of supplies. It didn't matter that we're two of the youngest Angels. He said we were the best people for the job.'

'Of course he was probably concerned about us too,' Awnya says. 'Being so young, I think he was worried that we might not be as capable as the others, and he wanted to find something to keep us busy, so we didn't feel out of place.'

'No way,' Cian barks. 'I keep telling you that's not the case. We train with the other guys and hold our own. Dr Oystein could send us on missions if he wanted. We just happen to be better than anyone else at doing this.'

Awnya catches my eye and we share a secret smile. Boys always want to think that they're able to do anything. We usually let them enjoy their fantasies. They're happier that way and do less whining.

'What sort of missions do the others go on?' I ask.

'Dull stuff mostly,' Cian huffs, and I decide to leave it there for the time being, as it's obviously a sore point for him.

We come to a closed door and Cian pushes it open. We step into one of County Hall's many huge rooms. There are six single beds arranged in a circle in the centre. The sheets and pillows on four of them have the crumpled look that shows they've been used recently. The other two have perfectly folded sheets and crease-free pillowcases.

There are three wardrobes, lots of shelving and two long dressing tables, one on either side of the room, with mirrors hanging on the walls above them, stools set underneath.

A girl is sitting on one of the stools, my age if not a bit older. She looks like an Arab, light brown skin, a plain blue robe and white headscarf. She's working on a model of the Houses of Parliament, made out of matchsticks. It looks pretty damn cool.

'Oh, hi, Ashtat,' Awnya says. 'We didn't know you were here.'

The girl half waves at us without looking round.

'This is Becky, but she prefers B,' Awnya presses on.

'Hush,' Ashtat murmurs.

'What's your problem?' I growl.

Ashtat scowls at me. 'I do not like being interrupted when I'm working on my models. You cannot know that, never having met me before, but the twins do.

78

They should not have admitted you until I was finished.'

'Like Awnya said, we didn't know you were here,' Cian protests. 'We thought you'd still be training with the others.'

'I tired of training early today,' Ashtat sniffs.

'Well, I'm here, so you'll have to live with it,' I tell her, determined to make my mark from the start. If I let her treat me like a dog now, I'll have to put up with that all the way down the line.

Ashtat raises an eyebrow but says nothing and returns to her model, carefully gluing another matchstick into place.

'She's OK when she's not working on a model,' Awnya whispers. 'Let's come back later.'

'No,' I say out loud. 'I'm staying. If she doesn't like that, tough. Which bed is mine?'

Awnya shows me to one of the spare beds. There's a bedside cabinet next to it. A few files for my teeth rest on top of the cabinet, along with the watches I was wearing, one of which was smashed to pieces in Trafalgar Square.

'Your hat's over there,' Cian says, pointing to a shelf. The shelf is blue, and so are the two shelves above it. 'The blue shelves are yours. You can stick anything you want on them, clothes, books, CDs, whatever. Half of that wardrobe –' he points to my left, '– is yours too. You're sharing with a guy called Jakob. He doesn't have much, so you should have plenty of room.'

'What about a bedroom of my own?' I ask.

Cian and Awnya shake their heads at the same time, the exact same way.

'Dr Oystein says it's important for us to share,' Cian says.

'It's the same for every Angel,' Awnya says. 'Nobody gets their own room.'

I frown. 'That's weird, isn't it?'

'It's meant to bring us closer together,' Awnya says.

'Plus it stops people arguing about who gets the rooms with the best views and most space,' Cian says.

'All right,' I sniff. 'I don't suppose I'll be using it much anyway. It's not like we need to sleep, is it?'

'No,' Cian says hesitantly. 'But Dr Oystein prefers it if we keep regular hours. We act as we did when we were alive. Most of us get up about seven every morning, do our chores, train, hang out, eat, whatever. Then we come to bed at midnight and lie in the dark for seven hours, resting.'

'It's good to have a routine,' Awnya says. 'It's comforting. You don't have to use your bed – nobody's going to force you – but if you want to fit in with the rest of us . . .'

'Sounds worse than prison,' I grumble, but I'm complaining just for the sake of it. Sinking on to the bed, I pick at my robe. 'What about clothes?'

'We thought you might want to choose your own,' Awnya says. 'We can get gear for you if you have specific requests. Otherwise we'll take you out later and show you round some of our favourite shops.'

'That sounds good,' I smile. 'I like to pick my own stuff.'

'We figured as much,' Awnya says smugly. 'We'll come and collect you in an hour or so.'

'What will I do until then?' I ask.

The twins shrug in unison.

'Get the feel of the place,' Cian says.

'Relax,' Awnya suggests.

'Keep quiet,' Ashtat lobs in.

I give her the finger, even though she can't see me, and slip on the watch that works, an ultra-expensive model that I picked up in the course of my travels. As the twins leave, I start to ask them for the correct time, in case the watch is wrong, but they're gone before I can.

I sigh and stare around the room, at the bed, the furniture, the silent girl and her matchstick model. Then, because I've nothing better to do, and because I'm a wicked sod, I start filing my teeth again, as loudly as I can, treating myself to a mischievous grin every time Ashtat twitches and shoots me a dirty look.

TEN

The twins take me over the river and into the Covent Garden area. True to their word, they know all the best shops, not just those with the coolest gear, but those with the least zombies. The living dead don't bother us much once they realise we're like them, but it's still easier to browse in places where they aren't packed in like sardines.

I choose several pairs of black jeans, a variety of dark T-shirts, a few jumpers and a couple of jackets. New sunglasses too, and a baseball cap with a skull design that I spot in a window, for those days when I don't

feel like the Australian hat which has served me well so far.

When it comes to shoes, the twins have a neat little device which screws into the material, making holes for the bones sticking out of my toes to jut through. They measure my feet and bore the holes with all the care of professional cobblers.

'I like it,' I grunt, admiring my new trainers.

'Dr Oystein invented that years ago,' Cian tells me, pocketing the gadget. 'He's like one of those crazy inventors you read about in comics.'

'Only not actually crazy,' Awnya adds.

'I don't know about –' I start to say, but a rapping sound on the shop window stops me.

We all instantly drop to our knees. There's another rap, a loud, clattering sound, but I can't see anyone.

'Do you think it's a revived?' I whisper.

'I don't know,' Cian says.

'I hope so,' Awnya croaks.

There's a long silence. I look around for another way out. Then there are two more raps on the glass. I spot a hand, low down and to the left, close to the open door. Another two raps. Then a series of short raps.

'I roll my eyes and stand. 'Very funny,' I shout.

'Careful, B,' Awnya moans. 'We don't know who it is.'

'But we know they have lousy taste in movies,' I snort. 'I recognise those raps. They're the theme tune from *Jaws*.'

'And what's wrong with that?' a girl challenges me, stepping into view outside. '*Jaws* is a classic.'

'The hell it is,' I reply. 'A boring old film with lousy special effects, and hardly anyone gets killed.'

'You don't know what you're talking about,' the girl says, stepping into the shop. Four teenage boys appear and follow her in. The girl smiles at the twins. 'Hey, guys, sorry if we frightened you.'

'We weren't frightened,' Cian says with a dismissive shake of his head, as if the very idea is offensive to him. 'We were excited. Thought we were going to see some action at last.'

'This is Ingrid,' Awnya introduces the girl. 'She's one of us.'

'I figured as much.' I cast an eye over the tall, blonde, athletic-looking girl. She's dressed in leathers, a bit like those the zom heads used to wear when they were tormenting reviveds.

'You must be B,' Ingrid says.

'Word travels fast,' I smile.

'Not that fast,' Ingrid says. 'You were in a Groove Tube for almost a month.'

My smile vanishes.

'What are you doing over here?' Cian asks. 'Are you on a mission?'

'Yeah,' Ingrid says.

'What sort of a mission?' I ask.

'The usual,' she shrugs. 'Looking for survivors. Searching for brains. Keeping an eye out for Mr Dowling or any other intruders.'

'We do this a lot,' one of the boys says. 'Not the most interesting of jobs, but it gets us out of County Hall.'

'Sounds like fun,' I lie, eager to see what they get up to. 'Can I come with you?'

'Absolutely not,' Ingrid says. 'You haven't been cleared for action by Master Zhang.'

'Aw, go on, Ingrid,' Cian pleads. 'If it's a normal mission, where's the harm? We can tag along too. We won't tell.'

'I don't know,' Ingrid says. 'This is serious business. If anything happened to you . . .'

'It won't,' Awnya says, as keen as her brother to get involved.

Ingrid checks with the rest of her pack. 'What do you guys think?'

They shrug. 'Doesn't matter to us,' one of them says.

'Three mugs to throw to Mr Dowling and his mutants if they turn up,' another guy smiles. 'Might buy us enough time to slip away.'

'Bite me,' I snap, and they all laugh.

'OK,' Ingrid decides. 'You can keep us company for a while. The experience will be good for you. But don't get in our way, do what we tell you and run like hell if we get into trouble.'

'How will we know?' Awnya asks nervously.

'Oh, trouble's easy to spot,' Ingrid says with an icy smile. 'It'll be when people start dying.'

ELEVEN

The Angels check the apartments above the shops, searching for survivors who might be holed up, or the corpses of people who died recently, whose brains might still be edible. They don't talk much, operating in silence most of the time, sweeping the rooms swiftly and efficiently.

One of the guys opens all of the doors. He has a set of skeleton keys and can deal with just about any lock that he encounters.

'That's Ivor Bolton,' Awnya whispers.

'Was he a thief when he was alive?' I ask.

'No. Master Zhang taught him.'

'Who's that?'

'Our mentor,' Awnya says. 'He trains every Angel. You'll meet him soon.'

'Do you all learn how to open locks?' I ask

'Only those who show a natural talent for it,' Cian says.

I stare at Ivor enviously. I hope I show that sort of promise. I'd love to be able to crack open locks and gain entrance to anywhere I wanted.

We explore more rooms, Ingrid and her team taking it slowly, carefully, searching for hiding places in wardrobes and under beds, tapping the walls for secret panels.

'Do you ever find people?' I ask as we exit a building and move on.

'Living people?' Ingrid shrugs. 'Rarely, around here. Most of the survivors in this area moved on or died ages ago. We dig up the occasional fresh corpse, but mainly we're checking that the buildings are clear, that potential enemies aren't setting up base close to County Hall.'

'What do you do if you find someone alive?' I ask.

She shrugs again. 'It depends on whether they want to come with us or not. Many don't trust us and leg it. If they stop and listen, we tell them about County Hall and offer to take them to it, and from there to somewhere safe.'

'That's one of the main things the Angels do,' Awnya chips in. 'We lead survivors out of London to secure camps in the countryside.'

'It's not as easy as it sounds,' Cian says.

'I bet not,' I grunt, thinking of all the difficulties I faced simply getting from the East End to here. 'Have you been on any of those missions yet?' I ask Ingrid.

'No,' she sighs. 'It's all been local scouting missions for us so far.'

'Long may they continue,' one of the boys mutters.

Cian scowls. 'You don't want to tackle the harder challenges?'

'We're not suicidal,' the boy snorts.

'Do you feel the same way?' I ask Ingrid.

She looks uncertain. 'Part of me wants to be a hero. But some of the Angels who go on the more dangerous missions don't make it back.'

We enter another building, a block of flats set behind a row of shops. We start up the stairs, the plan being to work our way down from the top. We're coming to the top of the fourth flight when Ingrid stops abruptly and presses herself against the wall.

'What's wrong?' I ask, as she makes some gestures to the boys in her team.

'I think I heard something,' she whispers.

'What?'

'I'm not sure. But we were here just a week ago. The place was deserted then.' She points to Ivor and another of the boys and sends them forward to check.

We wait in silence for the pair to return. I feel out of my depth. I want a weapon, something to defend myself with. Although, looking round at the others, I see that they don't have any weapons either. I want to ask them why they came out without knives or guns, but I don't want to be the one to break the silence.

There's no sign of Ivor and his partner. Ingrid gives it a few minutes, then signals to the other two boys to go and look for them.

'This is bad,' Cian groans quietly.

Ingrid fries him with a heated look and presses a finger to her lips.

The seconds tick away slowly. I keep checking the time on my watch. I want to push forward to find out what's happening, but I'm a novice here. I don't have the right to take control.

Ingrid waits a full five minutes, then swears mutely, just mouthing the word. She looks at me and the twins. Makes a gulping motion and licks her lips. Nods at us to backtrack and follows us down to the third floor.

'I don't know what's going on, but it can't be anything good,' she says quietly. 'Wait here for me, but no more than a couple of minutes. If I don't come back or shout to let you know that it's safe, return to County Hall and send others after us. *Do not* follow me up there, no matter what, OK?'

'I'm scared,' Awnya whimpers.

Cian hugs her, but he looks even more worried than his sister.

Ingrid casts a questioning glance at me.

'I'll take care of them,' I tell her.

She nods, then pads up the stairs.

Time seems to slow down even more. I fix my gaze on my watch, willing the hands to move faster, wanting Ingrid and her crew to appear and give us the all-clear. But when that doesn't happen, and the time limit passes, I look up at the twins.

'We're leaving?' Cian asks.

I shake my head. 'I can't. I've got to help them if I can. You guys go. Don't wait for me. Go now.'

'No,' Awnya says, horrified. 'Come with us, B. You can't go up there by yourself.'

'I have to. Don't argue. Get the hell out of here and tell the others what has happened.'

'But ...' She looks like she wants to cry, but being undead, she can't.

I start up as the twins start down. They go slowly, hesitantly, unable to believe that I'm following Ingrid and her team. I can barely believe it either. I must be mad. I hardly know them. I don't owe them anything. I should beat it with the twins.

But I don't. Maybe it's because I want to be a dumb hero. Or maybe it's because I don't think anything can be as scary as Mr Dowling and his mutants. Or maybe

96

it's the memory of Tyler Bayor, and what I did to him, that drives me on. Whatever the reason, I climb the steps, readying myself for battle, wondering what can have taken the Angels so swiftly and silently. I didn't even hear one of them squeak.

As I get to the top step and turn into the corridor, there's a sudden, piercing scream. It's Ingrid. I can't see her, but I hear her racing footsteps as she roars at me, 'Run, B, run!'

'Bloody hell!' I yell, and I'm off, tearing down the stairs like a rabbit, running for my life, panting as if I had lungs that worked.

I catch up with the twins. They're making sobbing sounds.

'What –' Awnya starts to ask.

'No questions,' I shout. 'Just run!'

We hit the ground floor in a frightened huddle and spill out on to the street. Our legs get tangled up and all three of us sprawl across the road. I curse loudly and push myself to my feet. I grab Awnya and pull her up. I'm reaching for Cian, to help him, when I hear . . .

. . . laughter overhead.

I pause, a familiar sickening feeling flooding my guts, and look up.

Ingrid and the boys are spread across the fourth-floor landing, and they're all laughing their heads off.

'Suckers!' Ivor bellows.

'Run, fools, run,' another of the boys cackles.

'Those sons of bitches,' I snarl.

'What's going on?' Cian asks, bewildered. 'Was it a joke?'

'Yeah,' I snap. 'And we fell for it.'

'Oh, thank God,' Awnya sighs. 'I thought they'd been killed.'

'Arseholes!' I roar at the five Angels on the landing, and give them the finger.

'You've got to be alert when you're out on a mission, B,' Ingrid cries. 'Wait. What's that behind us? No! Help us, B. Save us. There's a monster coming to …' She screams again, high-pitched and false.

'Yeah, laugh it up,' I shout. 'You won't be laughing when I stick my foot so far up your arse that …'

I shake my head, disgusted. But I'm disgusted at myself for falling for the trick, not at the Angels for pulling it. I should have known better.

'Come on,' I grunt at the twins. 'Let's leave them to their precious mission. We've better things to be doing back at County Hall.'

'That wasn't nice, Ingrid,' Awnya shouts.

'It was horrible,' Cian agrees.

'I know,' Ingrid says, looking contrite. Then she cackles again. 'But it was *fun!*'

We head off, pointedly ignoring those who made fools of us, but I stop when Ingrid calls to me.

'B!'

I turn stiffly, expecting another insult.

'All joking aside, we respect that you came back to try and help.'

'Yeah,' Ivor says. 'That took guts.'

'We'll be seeing you again soon on a mission, I think,' Ingrid says. 'But next time you'll be one of us, in on the joke, not the butt of it.'

'Whatever,' I sniff.

I carry on back towards County Hall with the twins, as if what Ingrid and Ivor said meant nothing to me, but it's a struggle to maintain my scowl and not smile with stupid pride all the way.

TWELVE

We head back over the river. We can laugh about what happened in the building by the time we've crossed the bridge.

'We've got to play a joke on them now,' Cian says. 'Not straight away, but within the next day or two. I'll think of something good. Maybe make them believe we're being attacked in the middle of the night, so that they panic and rush outside.'

There's a strange buzzing in the air as we step off the bridge and start towards County Hall. 'What's that?' I ask, grimacing as I draw to a halt.

'The speakers,' Awnya says. 'There are lots of them positioned around the area, to stop reviveds coming too close. They play this high-pitched noise all the time.'

'We'll slip past them as we get closer to the building,' Cian says. 'The speakers all point away from it, so we'll be fine once we're through.'

'How come I didn't hear it before?' I ask.

'Most of them have a small button that you can press to temporarily disable them,' Awnya says. 'I did that as we were leaving.'

'I didn't notice.'

Awnya shrugs. 'No reason why you should have.'

The twins show me the speakers as we get closer, and show me how to turn them off if I'm ever passing by myself. Then we head on into the building. They take me to my bedroom – I'm still not sure of the layout of the building, and where everything is – and I lay my gear on the shelves. There's no sign of Ashtat or any of the others.

The twins go off on their own for a while, leaving me to sort through my stuff and rest. Then they return and guide me to a dining room, close to the kitchen that I passed through earlier. Circular tables dot the room and groups of teenagers are clustered round them, chatting noisily. I do a quick count — there are just over thirty Angels.

'That's yours,' Awnya says, pointing at a table of three boys and Ashtat.

'Are those my room-mates?'

'Yes.'

'What are they like?'

Awnya shrugs. 'Ashtat can be moody, like you saw, but she's not so bad. Carl and Shane are OK. Jakob doesn't say much.'

'Which one's he?' I ask.

'The thin, bald one.'

'Carl's the dark-haired one,' Cian adds. 'Shane's the ginger.'

I wince, recalling the fate of the last redhead I knew, poor Tiberius.

'Go on over,' Awnya says. 'You don't want to eat with us. It'll look strange if you avoid them.'

I nod. 'Thanks for showing me around today.'

'That's our job,' Cian smirks.

'All part of the service,' Awnya grins.

They slip away to their own table and I stare at the teenagers seated at mine. Carl's dressed in designer gear, real flash. Shane's wearing a tracksuit, but with a gold chain dangling from his neck, like a wannabe rapper. Jakob is wearing a white shirt and dark trousers which look about two sizes too big for him. He's one of the unhealthiest-looking people I've ever seen, even by zombie standards. If I didn't know he was already dead, I'd swear he was at death's door.

And then there's Ashtat, dressed as she was when I saw her earlier. She spots me and says something to the others. They look at me curiously. I feel nervous, like I did on my first day of school.

'Sod it,' I mutter. 'They've got more reason to be scared of me than I have to be scared of them. I'm badass B Smith, and don't you forget it!'

With a scowl and a disinterested sniff, I cross the great expanse of the dining room, walking big, trying to act as if I belong.

'All right?' I grunt as I take a seat at the table.

Everyone nods but nobody says anything.

'I'm B.'

'We know,' Carl says, checking out my clothes. He nods again. I think I have his approval on the fashion front.

'Have the twins been taking care of you?' Shane asks.

'Yeah.'

'They're good at that.'

'Yeah.' There's an uncomfortable silence. Then I decide to wade straight in. 'Look, I don't like being told who my friends are. If it was up to me, I'd mix with the others, chat with different people, make up my own mind who I like and who I don't. I've already met Ingrid and her team, and I'd be happy to hang out with them. But I've been stuck with you lot for the time being, so we're just going to have to live with it.'

Carl laughs. 'You were never taught how to make a good first impression, were you?'

I shrug. 'This is me. I won't pretend to be something I'm not.'

'And what are you exactly?' Ashtat asks quietly.

'That's for you to work out,' I tell her, meeting her gaze and not looking away.

'We've got a live one here,' Shane chuckles.

'So to speak,' Carl adds, then sticks out a hand. 'Carl Clay. Kensington born and bred.'

'I was wondering about the posh accent,' I say as we shake hands.

'You should hear it when I'm trying to impress,' he grins.

I haven't had much contact with people like Carl. Kids from Kensington didn't wander over east too much in my day, unless to see some grungy art gallery or to go shopping in Canary Wharf. I don't like his accent, and I don't want to like him either, but his smile seems genuine. I'll give him a chance — just not much of one.

'Shane Fitz,' the ginger introduces himself. Shane doesn't offer to shake hands, just nods at me. I nod back. The chain-wearing Shane's the sort of bloke I'd have kicked the crap out of if our paths had crossed in the past. But times have changed. We're in the same boat now. As with Carl, I'll wait to pass judgement, see what he's made of.

'Ashtat Kiarostami,' the girl says softly, tilting her

head. 'I would like to apologise if I was rude to you earlier. I don't like to be disturbed when I'm working on my models and sometimes I react more sharply than intended.'

'Don't worry about it,' I sniff and look to the last of the four, the thin, bald kid with dark circles under his eyes.

'Jakob Pegg,' he wheezes and that's all I get out of him.

'So what's your story?' Carl asks, settling back in his chair. 'Where are you from? How were you killed? When did you revitalise?'

I tell them a bit about myself, the East End, the attack on my school, regaining consciousness in the underground complex. They're intrigued by that and pump me for more information. They haven't heard of anything like it before.

'I bet Dr Oystein was furious when you told him about that place,' Shane remarks.

'He knew about it already,' I reply. 'He said he had contacts there.'

Shane frowns. 'It can't have been anything to do with

Dr Oystein. He wouldn't approve of revitaliseds being imprisoned and experimented on.'

'Dr Oystein's approval doesn't mean much to the army,' Carl snorts. 'They do what they like. He has to keep them onside or they'll target us.'

'Bring 'em on,' Shane growls.

'Don't be stupid,' Ashtat chides him. 'They could level this place from the air. We would not even see who killed us.'

'So how'd you get out of there?' Carl asks as Shane seethes at the injustice of the world.

'Ever hear of a guy called Mr Dowling?'

Carl's eyes widen and Ashtat shivers. Shane pulls back from me, while Jakob leans forward, looking interested for the first time.

'I'll take that as a yes,' I say drily.

'We have heard rumours,' Ashtat murmurs, shivering again. 'Terrible rumours. If we could sleep, we would all have nightmares about him.'

'Speak for yourself,' Shane snorts, but he looks uneasy.

I tell them how the crazed clown and his mutants

invaded the complex and slaughtered many of the staff. But they didn't harm me or any of the other zom heads. Mr Dowling freaked me out – I wince as I recount how he opened his mouth and spat a stream of live spiders into my face – but he set me free once he'd made me tremble and shriek.

'I don't get it,' Shane frowns. 'Why did he free you? I thought Mr Dowling was our enemy.'

'He is,' Ashtat says. 'But he must have use for the living dead too. His mutants are clearly not enough for him. He wishes to recruit our kind also.'

'He should be so lucky,' Shane says witheringly. 'If he ever tries to sign me up for *Team Dowling*, I'll shove those spiders where the sun don't shine.'

'I'm sure that will make him quake in his boots,' Carl sneers.

'Do you know anything about Mr Dowling?' I ask before a fight breaks out between the snob and the chav.

'Not much,' Ashtat answers. 'And it is not our place to tell you what we know. Dr Oystein will do that when he returns.'

'You're all in love with that bloody doctor, aren't you?'

'He has given us a home,' Ashtat says. 'He has given our lives meaning. He has rescued us from an unliving hell and made us feel almost human. Of course we love him. You will too when you realise how fortunate you are to have been taken in by someone as accepting and forgiving as Dr Oystein.'

'I don't need his forgiveness,' I snort.

'No?' Ashtat asks quietly, eyeing me seriously.

I think about Tyler Bayor. Sister Clare of the Shnax. How I wasn't able to save Mark.

I go quiet.

'Grub's up!' someone calls out brightly. Looking up, I spot a smiling lady in a flowery apron entering the room, pushing a trolley loaded with bowls. It's the woman I noticed when Dr Oystein was first showing me around, the one who was scooping brains out of heads.

The Angels around me cheer loudly, as do all the others. The elegantly dressed dinner lady beams and takes a bow, then starts handing out the bowls.

'This is Ciara,' Ashtat says as she approaches our table. 'Ciara, this is Becky Smith, but she likes to be called B.'

'Pleasure to meet you, B,' Ciara says cheerfully. She looks more like a model than any dinner lady I ever met, with high cheekbones, carefully maintained hair, and clothes you'd only find in exclusive boutiques. Even the apron, white cap and green plastic gloves look more suited to a catwalk than a kitchen. But there's one thing about her that's far more extraordinary than her glamorous appearance.

She has a heartbeat.

'You're alive!' I gasp, the beat of her heart like a drum to my sensitive ears.

'Just about,' Ciara grins. 'But don't go thinking that means you can eat my brain. There should be more than enough for you there.'

She hands me a bowl filled with a familiar grey, gloopy substance. It's what the zom heads were fed in the underground complex, human brains mixed up in a semi-appetising way.

'For afters,' Ciara says, slamming a bucket down in

the middle of the table. She winks at me. 'Don't be offended if I don't stick around, but I can't stand all the vomiting. Come and have a chat with me later if you want. I used to work in Bow long ago, which – if I'm any judge of an accent – isn't too far from your neck of the woods. I'm sure we'll find plenty to talk about.'

Ciara sticks out a hand and pretends to ruffle my hair, only she doesn't quite touch me. Can't, since she's human and I'm not. I'd probably contaminate her if one of my hairs pierced her glove and stabbed into her flesh. I'm pretty sure that every cell of my body is toxic.

'I didn't expect to find living people here,' I remark as Ciara leaves.

'There aren't many,' Carl says, 'but we get a few passing through, and Ciara is a permanent fixture.'

'She was here when we first moved in,' Ashtat explains. 'She worked in one of the hotel restaurants. Dr Oystein calls her the queen of the dinner ladies. She's so stylish, isn't she? I asked her once why she chose to follow such a career. She said because she liked it, and we should all do what we like in life.'

'Isn't she afraid of being turned into one of us?' I ask.

'That cannot happen,' Ashtat says. 'If she was infected, she would become a revived. But no, she is not afraid. She feels safe around us. She knows we would not deliberately turn her. Of course it could happen accidentally if she fell against one of us and got scratched, but she is happy to take that risk. She says there are no guarantees of safety anywhere in this world now.'

'But if she is ever turned, God help the bugger who does it to her,' Shane growls. 'I don't care if it's an accident — if anyone hurts Ciara, I'll come after them with everything I have.'

'You're my hero,' Carl simpers. 'Now shut up and eat.'

Shane scowls but digs in as ordered.

I tuck into the gruel, not bothering with the spoon which Ciara supplied, just tipping it straight into my mouth from the bowl. I used to think it was disgusting, but having had to scoop brains out of skulls to survive since leaving the underground complex, I'm less fussy now.

Jakob is first to finish — he doesn't eat all of his

gruel – and he reaches for the bucket and turns aside, sticking a couple of fingers down his throat. The rest of us follow his example when we're ready and the room comes alive with the sound of a few dozen zombies throwing up.

The children of the night — what sweet music we make!

THIRTEEN

Nobody says much for a while after we've finished eating and puking. We all look a bit sheepish. It's not easy doing this in public, even for those who've been living together as Angels for months. It feels like having a dump in front of your friends. I've done a lot of crazy things over the years, but I drew the line at that! Yet here we are, all thirty plus of us, looking like we've been caught with our pants down around our ankles.

Ashtat pulls something out of a pocket, closes her hands over it and starts to pray silently. I roll my eyes at the boys and make a gagging motion, but they don't laugh. When Ashtat finishes and unclasps her hands, I see that the object is a crucifix.

'What are you doing with that?' I ask.

'Praying.'

'With a cross? Don't you guys use ... I don't know ... but not a cross. Those are for us lot.'

'*Us lot?*' Ashtat repeats icily.

'Christians.'

'What makes you think I'm not a Christian?'

I snort. 'You're an Arab. There aren't any Christians in the Middle East.'

'Actually there are,' Ashtat says tightly. 'Quite a few, for your information.'

'I'm not talking about people who go there on pilgrimage,' I sniff.

'Nor am I,' she says. 'I'm talking about Arab Christians.'

'Pull the other one,' I laugh.

Ashtat raises an eyebrow. 'You don't think you can be both an Arab and a Christian?'

'Of course not. You're one or the other.'

'Really?' she jeers. 'So you think that all Arabs are Muslims?'

'Yeah,' I mutter, although I'm getting the sinking feeling that I'm on a hiding to nothing. 'You all worship Allah.'

'And who is Allah?' she presses.

'Your god.'

'No,' she barks. '*Our* god. God and Allah are one and the same. Assuming you believe in God.'

'Well, I'm not religious, but if I did believe, it would be in God, not Allah.'

'As I just told you,' she says, 'Allah *is* God. Our religions have the same roots. Muslims believe in the Old Testament and they revere Christ, Mary and all the saints that Christians do.'

I scratch my head and stare at her, lost for words.

'You don't know anything about Islam, do you?' she says.

'Not really, no,' I admit grudgingly.

Ashtat starts to laugh, then grimaces. 'I'm sorry. I should not mock you for being ignorant. In my experience, most of your people knew nothing about mine. We were just potential terrorists in your eyes.'

I want to protest but I can't, because it's the truth.

'I'm not going to give you a history lesson,' Ashtat goes on. 'If you are truly interested, you can look up the facts yourself. But Muslims and Christians – Jews too – all started out in the same place and believe in the same God. We branched along the way, but at our core we are the same.

'I'm Muslim,' she continues, 'but one of my grandmothers was Christian. She converted when she came to this country and married my grandfather, but she told her children and grandchildren about her old beliefs and encouraged us to respect Christianity. The Virgin Mary was her favourite and I often say a prayer to her, thinking of my grandmother, especially in these troubled times.'

Ashtat stops and waits for me to respond. I can only gawp at her. It's like I've been told that the Earth actually is flat or the moon truly is made of cheese.

'Why did your people hate us if that's the case?' Shane asks. This is obviously news to him too.

'Why did *your* people hate *us*?' Ashtat retorts.

'Because of September the tenth and all the other crap,' Shane says.

120

'You mean September the eleventh,' Carl sighs, rolling his eyes.

'What about the Crusades?' Ashtat counters. 'Western Christians tried to wipe out my people, to steal our land and treasures. Later, in the twentieth century, you divided up our nations as it suited you, to govern us as you saw fit. You . . .' She shakes her head. 'We could argue about this forever, but it would not do any good. I don't hate anyone or blame anyone or see myself as being part of any army except the army of the Angels. The old grudges seem ridiculous now that the world has changed so much.'

'You're the one who started the argument,' I pout.

'I was not arguing,' she contradicts me. 'I was simply pointing out a matter of fact, in response to your assertion that Arabs could not also be Christians.'

'All right. I stand corrected. Happy now?'

'Yes,' Ashtat says, putting away her crucifix.

'I didn't mean any harm,' I add softly.

She smiles. 'I know. Forget about it.'

'My dad . . .' I consider telling them how I was raised, about my racist father, what happened with

Tyler, how I'm trying to be different. But before I can decide how to start, a Chinese guy enters the dining room and claps loudly.

All conversation comes to an immediate halt. Everyone rises and bows. The newcomer waits a moment, then bows smoothly in return. When he straightens, he looks around, spots me and comes across.

He's a bit taller than me, although not a lot older, maybe five or six years my senior, dressed in jeans and a white T-shirt. No shoes. Bones jut out of his toes and fingers. They've been carefully trimmed into dagger-like tips.

He stops in front of me. I'm the only person still sitting. I glance at the others but they don't look at me. Their gazes are fixed dead ahead.

'I am Master Zhang,' he says softly. 'In future you will stand and bow when you see me.'

'Why?' I snap.

His right hand flickers and before I can react, his fingers are tightening round my throat. I slap at his arm and try to pull free, but he holds firm.

'Because I will kill you if you do not,' he says without changing tone.

'Don't ... need ... breath,' I growl. 'You ... can't ... choke ... me.'

'No. But I can rip your head from your neck and dig into your brain. I could do it now. I would not even need to alter my grip. Do you doubt that?'

I stare into his dark brown eyes – one of them is badly bloodshot – and shake my head stiffly.

'Good,' he says, releasing me. 'That is a start. Now you will stand, bow and say my name.'

I want to tell him to get stuffed, but I've a feeling my head would be sent rolling across the floor before I got to the end of the insult. I don't think this guy plays games, that he's someone you can push to a certain point. You show him respect or he rips your apart, simple as that.

Pushing my chair back, I stand, bow and mutter as politely as I can, 'Master Zhang.'

'Good,' he says again, then turns to face Carl. 'You will bring her to me when you are finished here. I will test her.'

'Yes, Master Zhang,' Carl says, bowing again.

Zhang leaves without saying anything else. Once he's gone, the Angels sit and conversation resumes as if we were never interrupted.

I rub my throat and glare at the others. 'You could have warned me,' I snarl.

Carl waves away my accusation. 'We all have to go through that. Master Zhang likes to make his own introductions.'

'Do you really think he would have ripped my head off?' I ask.

'If you were dumb enough to assume he was joking, yes,' Carl says. 'But so far nobody's made that mistake. Even Shane knew better than to give Master Zhang any grief.'

'I'd like to see him tear someone's head off though,' Shane says. He shoots me a quick look. 'I was hoping *you* might talk back to him, just to see what he'd do.'

'Good to know you have my back if things ever get ugly,' I snarl. For a few seconds I consider walking out the door and leaving — in some ways this place is just as bad as the underground complex where I was held prisoner. But where would I go? Who could I turn to? Grumbling darkly, I sit down like the rest of them. 'So that guy's your mentor?' I ask, recalling what Awnya said when she mentioned him.

'Yes,' Ashtat says. 'He teaches us how to fight and fend for ourselves, so that we are ready for the missions on which we are sent.'

'Just him?'

'Yes. He is the only tutor we need.'

'And the test he mentioned?'

Ashtat snickers. 'Every Angel trains with Master Zhang, but some are deemed more worthy of his attention than others. He will take your measure when you spar with him. If he is impressed, you will train to join the likes of us on life-or-death missions.'

'If you disappoint him,' Carl says, 'you'll end up rooting through shops for supplies with the twins.'

'Or mixing up brains with Ciara to put in the gruel,' Shane giggles.

'It's time to find out if you're a lion or a lamb,' Ashtat says.

'I'm no bloody lamb,' I growl.

She purses her lips. 'No, I do not think that you are.' Then her expression softens and she adds hauntingly, 'Although if you are cleared to come on missions with us, you might end up wishing that you were.'

FOURTEEN

When everyone's had their fill, they stack up the bowls and leave them on the tables, then file out of the dining room. Carl tells me to accompany him to the gym for my test with Master Zhang. I expect the others to come with us, but they head off to do their own thing.

'This won't be the gladiatorial showdown of the year,' Carl smirks, noting my disappointment.

'What do you mean?'

'It's not going to be some amazing duel, with you pushing Master Zhang all the way. The test for newbies is pretty boring. That's why no one's interested.'

'Maybe I'll surprise you,' I grunt.

'No,' he says. 'You won't.'

Carl takes me by the swimming pool on our way. A couple of Angels are doing laps, moving faster than any Olympic swimmer, like a pair of sharks following a trail of blood.

'Can you swim?' Carl asks.

'Yeah.'

'You're free to train here whenever you want,' he says. 'But make sure you plug up your nostrils and ears — water will lodge if you don't. And keep your mouth firmly shut. Liquids slip down our throats easily enough, but they're a real pain to get rid of. Trust me, unless you like wearing nappies, you don't want to go sloshing around with a few litres of water inside you.'

'I'll bear that in mind.'

The gym is fairly standard, cross-trainers, rowing machines, weights and so on. Several Angels are working out, some under the gaze of Master Zhang, others by themselves.

Master Zhang ignores me for a few minutes, studying a girl as she performs a series of gymnastic routines in front of a dummy that must have been brought here from a shop. Each spin or twirl ends with a flick of a hand or foot to the dummy's head or torso. She's already chipped away at a lot of it, and keeps on tearing in, cracking it, knocking chunks loose, ignoring the cuts and nicks she's picking up.

'Keep going until there is nothing left to destroy,' Master Zhang says to the girl, then strides for the door, nodding at Carl and me to follow.

He leads us to a bare room that looks like it was once a conference room for high-flying businessmen. Any chairs and tables have been removed, though there are still some whiteboards on the walls.

'Each revitalised is different,' Master Zhang says, wasting no time on chit-chat. 'Our bodies react uniquely when we return to life. There are similarities common to all – extra strength and speed – but nobody can judge the extent of their abilities until they test themself. Physical build is not a factor. Some of us have great potential. Others do not.

'We can fine-tune whatever skills we possess, but if you are found lacking at this stage, you will forever be limited by the restraints of your body. When you died, you lost the capacity to improve on what nature provided you with. In short, your response to today's test will decide your role within the Angels for the next few thousand years. So I suggest you apply yourself as best you can.'

Master Zhang marches me to one end of the room, then tells me to make a standing jump. I crouch, tense the muscles in my legs, then spring forward like a frog. I hurtle almost two-thirds of the way across the room, far further than any human could have ever jumped. I'm delighted with myself, but when I look at Master Zhang, he makes a so-so gesture.

'Carl,' he says and Carl copies what I did, only he sails past me and bounces off the wall ahead of us.

'Does that mean I've failed?' I ask bitterly.

'No,' Master Zhang said. 'It simply means that if someone is required to leap across a great distance – for instance, from the roof of one building to another – we will choose Carl or another like him.'

Next we step out into the corridor and I perform a running jump. I do better this time, although still nowhere near what Carl can do. Then Master Zhang times me racing up and down. He's pleased with my speed. 'Not the fastest by any means, but quicker than many.'

We step back into the room and Master Zhang tests my sense of balance by having me stand in a variety of uncomfortable positions and hold the pose as long as I can. Then he tests my reflexes by lobbing small, hard balls at me. Again he's happy with my response, but far from overwhelmed.

We return to the gym and he tries me out with weights. I come up short on this one. Others are lifting weights around me and I can see that I don't match up. I lift far more than I could have when I was alive, but ultimately I fall low down the pecking order.

'Do not look so upset,' Master Zhang says as I step away from the weights, feeling defeated. 'I am by no means the strongest person here, but that has never worked against me. I taught myself how to deal with stronger opponents many years ago and my foes have yet to get the better of me.'

'Have a lot of foes, do you?' I laugh.

'Yes,' he says simply, not bothering to elaborate.

Then it's back to the conference room, where Master Zhang has me face him. Carl watches from a spot near the door, grinning eagerly.

'This is the part you have probably been looking forward to,' Master Zhang says. 'I am going to test your sharpness and wit. I want you to try to hit me, first with your fists, then with your feet. You can use any move you wish, a punch, chop, slap, whatever.'

'Shouldn't we be in karate or boxing gear for this sort of thing?' I ask.

'No. We do not wear special clothes when we fight in the world outside, so why should we wear them here? I want to see how you will perform on the streets, where it matters.'

With a shrug, I eye up Master Zhang, then jab a fist at his nose. He shimmies and my fist whistles through thin air. I expected as much, and also guessed the way he would move, so even while he's ducking, I'm bringing up my other fist to hit him from the opposite side.

Master Zhang grabs my arm and stops my fist short of its target.

'Good,' he says, releasing me. 'Again.'

I spend the next ten minutes trying to strike him with my fists, then ten trying to hit him with my feet. I fare better with my feet than fists, connecting with his shoulders and midriff a number of times, and once – sweetly – with the side of his face. I don't cause any damage but I can tell he's impressed.

'Rest a while,' he says, taking a step back.

'I didn't think zombies needed rest.'

'Even the living dead need rest,' he says. 'We are more enduring than we were in life, but our bodies do have limits. If we demand too much of ourselves, it affects our performance. We can struggle on indefinitely, sluggishly, but our battles need to be fought on our terms. It is not enough to be dogged. We must be incisive.'

'Who do we fight?' I ask. 'Mr Dowling and his mutants? Reviveds? The army?'

'Dr Oystein will answer your questions,' Master Zhang says. 'I am here merely to determine how useful you might be to us and to help you make the most of your talents.'

Master Zhang spends the next ten minutes throwing punches and kicks at me. I manage to duck or block many of them, but plenty penetrate and by the end of the session I'm stinging all over. But it's a good kind of pain and I don't mind.

After opening up a small cut beneath my right eye, Master Zhang says, 'That will be enough. Return tomorrow. I want to see how your cuts moss over.'

'What do you mean?' I ask.

'We cannot heal as we could when we were alive,' he explains. 'Moss grows in places where we are cut, but it sprouts more thickly in some than in others. If the moss grows thinly over your cuts, you will continue to lose blood when you fight, which will affect your performance, making you of little use to us.'

'Nothing wrong with my moss,' I say confidently. 'Look, it's already stitching the wound closed, I can feel it.' I tilt my head backwards, so that he can see.

Master Zhang smiles thinly. 'I believe that it is. But as I said, come back to see me tomorrow, and we will test it then.'

'Assuming the moss grows thickly,' I call after him as

he turns to leave, 'how did I do on the rest of the tests? Am I good enough to be a proper Angel with Carl and the others?'

Master Zhang pauses and casts a slow look over me with his bloodshot left eye. I feel like I'm being X-rayed.

'Physically, yes, my feeling is that you are, although there are a few more tests that you must complete before we can say for certain. Mentally?' He looks unsure. 'Most living people fear death more than anything else, but our kind need not, since we have already died. So tell me, Becky Smith, what do you fear more than anything else now?'

I think about telling him that I don't fear anything, but that wouldn't be the truth. And I think about saying that I fear Mr Dowling, Owl Man and the mutants, but while I'm certainly scared of the killer clown and his strange associates, they're not the ones who gnaw away at my nerves deep down. I'm sure that if I'm not totally honest with Master Zhang, he'll pick up on the deception and it will go against me. So, even though I hate having to admit it, I tell him.

'I'm afraid of myself,' I croak, lowering my gaze to hide my shame. 'I've done some bad things in the past, and I'm afraid, if I don't keep a close watch on myself every single day, that I might do even worse.'

There's a long silence. Then Master Zhang makes a small clucking sound. 'I think you will fit in here,' he says.

And that marks the end of the first round of tests.

FIFTEEN

'I told you it wouldn't be exciting,' Carl says as we head back to our room.

I grunt.

'You'll have to get used to the boredom,' he continues. 'We spend most of our time training. It sounds like it will be great, learning how to fight, and there *are* times when I learn a new move and it feels amazing. But for the most part it's pretty dull.'

There's no one in our room when we get there. Carl changes his shirt – there wasn't anything wrong with the old one, he just wants to try something new – and we head to the front of the building, out on to a large terrace overlooking the river. Carl doesn't stop to admire the view, but hurries down the stairs and along the path.

'Are we going to the London Dungeon?' I ask, spotting a sign for it.

Carl gives me an odd look. 'Isn't the world grisly enough for you as it is?'

'But the Dungeon's fun,' I laugh.

'It used to be,' he agrees. 'Not so much now that there aren't any actors to bring the place to life. We sometimes train down there, but we don't really make use of it otherwise. It's not a fun place to hang out.'

'Do the rides still work?' I ask.

'Yes,' he says.

'Come on. Let's try them.'

'Maybe later,' he says, then heads for the old arcade centre. I could go and explore the Dungeon by myself, but I don't want to be alone so, with a scowl, I follow him.

Most of the video games in the arcade still seem to be operational, but although a handful of Angels are hanging around, nobody's playing. That seems strange to me until I recall my advanced sense of hearing and the way bright lights hurt my eyes. I guess half an hour on a video game in my current state would be about as much fun as sticking my hand into a food blender.

Our lot are bowling. They have the lanes to themselves. Jakob is taking his turn as we approach. He knocks down the four standing pins and gets a spare.

'Nice one,' Shane says.

Jakob only shrugs. I've never seen anyone who looks as miserable as this guy. I wonder what it would take to make him smile.

'How did the test go?' Ashtat asks as we slip in beside her.

'I aced it. Master Zhang said I was the best student he'd ever seen.'

'Sure,' she drawls. 'I bet he got down on his knees and worshipped you.'

We grin at each other. We got off on the wrong foot, but I'm starting to warm to the Muslim girl, which is something I never thought I'd hear myself admit.

Shane hits the gutter and swears.

'You're lucky Master Zhang wasn't here to see that,' Carl tuts.

'Why?' I ask. 'Don't tell me he's a master bowler too.'

'It's part of our training,' Shane sighs, waiting for his ball to return. 'He says bowling is good for concentration. Our eyes aren't as sharp as they were, and no amount of drops will ever change that. We have to keep working on our hand to eye coordination.'

'Eye to hand,' Carl corrects him.

'Whatever,' Shane mutters and throws again. This time he knocks down seven pins but he's not happy. He flexes his fingers and glares at them as if they're to blame.

Ashtat throws and gets a strike. Jakob steps up next, then pauses and offers me the ball.

'Don't you want to finish the game?' I ask.

'No,' he whispers. 'It doesn't matter.'

I take the ball from him and test the holes. They're too small for my fingers – I cast a quick glance at Jakob and note how unnaturally thin he is – so I put it back and find one that fits. I take aim, step up and let the ball rip.

It shoots down the lane faster than I would have thought possible and smashes into the pins, sending them scattering in every direction. A few of them shatter and go flying across the adjacent lanes.

'Bloody hell!' I gasp, shocked and dismayed. 'I'm sorry. I didn't mean to . . .'

I stop. The others are laughing. Even Jakob is smiling slightly. Shane high-fives the thin, bald kid, then slaps my back. 'Don't worry. That happens to most of us the first time.'

'We're stronger than we look,' Ashtat says. 'We have to learn to control our strength. That's another of the reasons we practise here.'

'You could have told me that before I threw,' I say sourly.

'It wouldn't have been as funny then,' Carl giggles.

'No,' I smile. 'I guess it wouldn't.'

We move to another lane while Jakob clears up the mess and replaces the pins. It takes me a while to get the balance right – I throw the first few balls too softly, then hit the gutters when I lob more forcefully – but eventually I find my groove. It's tricky to be accurate because of my weak eyesight, but I can compensate for that by throwing a bit harder than I did when alive.

After a couple of games – I finish last the first time, but fourth in the next game, ahead of a disgusted Shane – we spill out of the arcade. Night has fallen and dark clouds drift across the sky. I suggest the Dungeon again, but the others say they want to go on the London Eye. I'm curious to see what the city looks like now from up high, so I don't argue.

We step into one of the pods and rise. I turn slowly as we ascend, taking in the three hundred and sixty degree view. As I'm turning, I spot an Angel sitting on the bench in the middle of a pod on the opposite side of the big wheel, staring solemnly out over the river.

'What's up with that guy?' I ask.

'He's a lookout,' Carl says. 'There's always an Angel on duty in the Eye, in touch with a guard inside County Hall, in case we get attacked by Mr Dowling and his mutant army. They use walkie-talkies — mobile phones don't work any more.'

'I noticed that,' I frown. 'Any idea why not?'

'It's the end of the world,' Carl says. 'Lots of things don't work.'

'I know, but I thought mobiles would be all right, since they operate through satellites.'

'You thought wrong,' Carl sniffs. 'That's why we rely on the walkie-talkies. You'll be posted to a pod once you settle in. We all have to take our turn, even the twins and those who don't come on missions.'

'Except for One-eyed Pete,' Ashtat says.

'Obviously,' Carl replies.

I whistle, impressed. 'There's really an Angel called One-eyed Pete?'

Carl and Ashtat gaze at me serenely and I realise I've taken the bait, hook, line and sinker.

'All right,' I growl as they burst out laughing. 'I'm an idiot. I admit it. Just throw me off this thing when we get to the top and have done with me.'

We chat away as the pod glides upwards, admiring the view over County Hall, looking down on the roof and into the courtyards. I try to spot the room where the Groove Tubes are, but it's hard to be sure.

'I came up here a few times with my mum and

dad when I was younger,' I mumble, remembering happier days when the world wasn't a nightmarish place.

'What happened to them?' Ashtat asks quietly.

'I don't know. I think Dad might have made it out. Mum . . .' I shake my head, wondering again about her, hoping she's alive, but not able to believe that she is. And Dad? Well, it's kind of the opposite with him. I'm pretty sure he slipped away, but part of me hopes he didn't, that he paid for what he made me do to Tyler. But I don't *want* to feel that way. He's my dad, and as much as I hate him for what he is – what he always was – I love him too.

'How about the rest of you?' I ask. 'Did you all lose family?'

'Yes,' Ashtat says. 'Parents, brothers, sisters . . .'

'A girlfriend,' Shane adds morosely.

'A boyfriend,' Carl sighs, then winks at a startled Shane. 'Only joking.'

'You'd better be,' Shane huffs. 'I'm not sharing a room with you if not.'

Carl fakes a gasp. 'Hark at the homophobe! Just for

that, I'm going to convert. Come here, you big sap, and give me a kiss.'

They wrestle and stumble around the pod, Carl laughing, Shane cursing. The rest of us look on wearily.

'Boys never change, do they?' I note.

'Sadly, no,' Ashtat murmurs. 'They might have lost their carnal appetites, but that won't stop them being bothersome little pests.'

'Lost their . . .? Oh yeah, I forgot about that.'

Apparently zombies can't get down and dirty — none of the necessary equipment is in working order. Apart from snogging – which probably isn't much fun with a dry tongue and cold lips – there's not much we can do.

Shane and Carl break apart. Both are grinning. Then Carl's expression darkens as he recalls what we were talking about.

'I went to the offices where my father used to work once I'd revitalised. I found him there. He's a revived now. I thought about killing him but I didn't dare, just in case anyone ever discovered a cure for them.'

'You know that won't happen,' Ashtat says sympathetically.

'Yeah, but still ...'

'Your dad might revitalise,' I say, trying to cheer him up.

Carl squints at me. 'What are you talking about?'

'Well, we recovered our senses, so maybe he will too.'

'He can't,' Carl says. 'He wasn't vaccinated.'

'What?' I frown.

'Leave it.' Ashtat stops Carl before he can continue. 'Dr Oystein will explain it when he returns.'

'I'm getting sick of hearing that,' I growl. 'What is he, the bloody keeper of all secrets? Are you afraid the world will go up in flames if you tell me something behind his back?'

'It's just simpler if he tells you,' Ashtat says calmly. 'He's used to explaining. If we tried, we might confuse you.'

'At least you admit that you don't know what the hell you're talking about,' I mutter, then cast an eye over Jakob who, as usual, is standing silently by the rest of us. 'What about you, skeleton boy? Did zombies eat your nearest and dearest, or did they leave Ma and Pa Addams alone?'

Jakob stares at me uncertainly, then gets the reference. 'Oh. I see. I look like one of the Addams Family. Very funny.'

'You bitch,' Ashtat snarls.

'What?' I snap. 'Aren't we allowed to have a go at skinheads any more?'

'You don't think he shaved himself, do you?' she asks.

'Well, yeah, of course. I mean why else . . .?'

I stop and wince. How dumb am I? Pale skin. Bald. Dark circles under his eyes. Skinny in an unhealthy way.

'You've got cancer, haven't you?' I groan.

'Yes,' Jakob says softly. 'It was terminal. I was close to the end. I had maybe a few weeks left to live. Then I was bitten. Now I'm going to be like this forever.'

'Is the cancer still active?' I ask. 'Will it carry on eating you up?'

'No,' he sighs. 'But it hasn't gone away. It still hurts. I can ignore the pain and function normally when I focus, which is why I'm allowed to go on missions, but

150

the rest of the time I feel weak, tired and disoriented. It's why I often seem spaced out.'

'I'm sorry. Really. I wouldn't have had a go at you if I'd known.'

He waves away my apology. 'It doesn't matter. Nothing that you said could hurt me. Nobody could. Not after . . .'

He stops and I think he's going to clam up again. But then he continues, his voice the barest of whispers, so that even with my sharp ears I have to strain to catch every word.

'I'd come to London with my parents and younger sister. One last visit. Nobody phrased it that way but we all knew. Our final day out together. Mum and Dad took time off work, even though they couldn't afford to — they were struggling to make ends meet, having spent so much on me over the last few years.

'We got delayed on our way down, so we had to cut out some of the things we'd planned to do. In the end we went to Trafalgar Square first. I loved the lions, the fountains, looking up at the National Gallery.'

I consider telling him what happened the last time I

was in Trafalgar Square, but I don't dare interrupt him in case he goes silent again.

'We had lunch in the crypt in St Martin-in-the-Fields. I had a Scotch egg. I knew it would make me sick – my stomach couldn't handle rich food – but I didn't care. It was sort of my last supper. I wanted it to be special.' He smiles fleetingly. 'That's how bad things get when you're that close to death. A Scotch egg becomes something special.'

Jakob retreats from the window and sits on the bench. Rests his hands on his knees and carries on talking. No one else makes a sound. If we could hold our breath – if we had breath to hold – we would.

'I was one of the first to be attacked when zombies spilled into the crypt. In a way that was a mercy. I didn't have to witness the madness and terror which must have surely followed.

'I was still in the crypt when I regained my senses weeks later. I'd made a base there, along with dozens of others. I'd fashioned a cot out of a few of the corpses. I suppose it was a bed cum larder, as I'd eaten from them too. I know that because I was eating when I revitalised, digging my fingers into a skull, scraping out a few dry, tasteless scraps of brain.

'It was my sister's skull,' he says, and the most horrible thing about it is that his tone doesn't change. It's like he's telling us the time. 'My mum and dad were there too. Well, in my dad's case it was just his head. I couldn't find his body. I did search for it but . . .'

Jakob pauses, then decides to stop. He lowers his head and starts to massage his neck. Nobody says anything.

Without discussing it, we spread out around the pod, giving Jakob some privacy. We stare at the river and the buildings, smoke rising into the air from a number of places, corpses strewn everywhere, abandoned boats and cars, paths and roads stained with blood, black in the dim night light.

I think about asking Ashtat if I can borrow her cross. But I don't. And it's not because I don't want to be a hypocrite and say a prayer to a God I barely believe in. It's because I figure what's the point in saying any prayers for this broken, bloodied city of the ungodly dead?

SIXTEEN

Carl wasn't joking about training being boring. Over the next three days I perform the same routines over and over — swim (having carefully plugged up my nose and ears), work out in the gym and get thrown around the hollow conference room by the stone-faced Master Zhang.

'It is important that you learn how to fall correctly,' he says when I complain after being slammed down hard on the floorboards for the hundredth time. 'In a fight, you will often be thrown or knocked over. If you can cushion your landing, you will be in a better position to carry on.'

'How long will I have to do this?' I grumble, rubbing my bruised shoulders. I'm beginning to wish he'd ruled me unfit for active service.

'Until I am satisfied,' he says and hurls me over his shoulder again.

I'm keen to learn all sorts of cool moves, and disgusted by what I consider a waste of my time, so I leave the sessions with a face like thunder, but Ashtat tells me I have to be patient. They all had to endure this to begin with.

'Master Zhang wants to turn you into a fighting machine,' she explains. 'That isn't a simple task. You should be thankful he's spending so much time on you, even if it is only to throw you around. If he didn't consider you worthy, he would not be proceeding so diligently with you.'

I know she's right, but it's hard to maintain my interest and temper. I was never the most patient of girls. Maybe that's why I didn't have a boyfriend — I couldn't be bothered putting in all the time and effort required.

If I'd come to Master Zhang when I was human, I doubt I'd have stuck with him more than a day. I definitely wouldn't have made it past the second. But things are different now. It's not like I have more attractive options. If I don't play ball here, I can go off by myself, regress and become a shambling revived, or maybe hook up with Mr Dowling and his merry band of mutants. Hardly the sort of career prospects that young girls around the world dream about.

At least I get on pretty well with my room-mates. They're not the sort I would have been friends with in my previous life, but they're not a bad bunch. They do their best to help me find my feet, show me round County Hall, give me tips like how to groom the bones sticking out of my fingers and toes.

I haven't spoken to many of the other Angels. I've picked up names here and there, and I know a few to nod to in the gym and pool – such as Ingrid and her crew – but I haven't tried to bond with any of them. I'm still not sure if this place is for me, and won't know for certain until I've had a chance to chat with Dr Oystein again. If I don't like what I hear, and decide that I'm better off out of it, I don't want the added aggro of having to leave friends behind.

157

On the afternoon of the fourth day, after lunch, when I have free time on my hands, I head down to the lab with the Groove Tubes to catch up with Reilly, something I've been meaning to do since our first reunion.

The soldier isn't in the lab, nor is Rage, who must have been fished out not long after I was. I get an angry feeling in my gut when I spot the empty Tube, recalling the way Rage threw the rest of the zom heads to the lions, how he killed Dr Cerveris. I'm uneasy too — I don't trust Rage. It wouldn't surprise me if he popped up behind me and dug a knife into the back of my skull.

I ask around and track down Reilly to the kitchen where Ciara works. Reilly and the dinner lady are talking while she washes up. As far as I'm aware, they're the only two humans here, so I guess they feel closer to one another than to the cannibalistic zombies they serve.

'Hey,' Reilly says when he spots me. 'I was wondering when you'd come looking for me.'

'What made you think I would?' I snort.

'I've always known you had a crush on me,' he grins.

'Not if you were the last guy in the world,' I jeer, hopping up on to a table across from the pair and letting my legs dangle. 'Isn't there a dishwasher for that?' I ask Ciara as she scrubs another plate.

'I prefer washing by hand,' she says cheerfully. 'It passes the time and it keeps my mind off . . . other matters.'

Her shoulders shudder slightly and I don't ask any more questions. I'm sure, like any other survivor in this post-apocalyptic city, that she has memories she'd rather not dwell on.

'Go on then,' I say to Reilly. 'Tell me how you came to be here.'

He shrugs. 'There's no big story. Josh and the others who hadn't been killed by the clown and his mutants pulled out of the underground complex in the wake of the assault. I'd had doubts about the place from the beginning. What I saw that day – the way the reviveds and revitaliseds were executed like rabid animals – helped make up my mind. I wanted out, so I walked away while they were evacuating. I doubt if anyone missed me. If they did, they probably assumed I was killed or converted by a stray zombie.'

'Took you long enough to see them for what they were,' I sniff.

Reilly sighs. 'Things aren't black and white any more. They never were, I suppose, but there used to be law and order, right and wrong. Now it's all chaos. I don't think Josh or Dr Cerveris were bad guys. They were trying to uncover answers, to figure out a way to put the world back on track. I didn't approve of how they went about it, but if they'd cracked the zombie gene and come up with a way to rid the world of the living dead . . .'

'They'd have been your heroes?' I sneer.

'Yeah,' he says. 'You've got to remember, *you're* the enemy. Dr Oystein is doing an incredible job, and I admire how his Angels have dedicated themselves to helping the living. But you're all part of the problem. Dr Oystein acknowledges that, so it's not like I'm being disrespectful. The world has been torn apart by a war between the living and the dead, and even though you guys are on my side, I can't trust you. One scrape of those bones, if I stumbled and you instinctively reached out to grab me, and I'm history.'

I frown. 'So why swap Josh for Dr Oystein?'

'I think he can do more than Josh could,' Reilly says. 'He knows more about what makes you lot tick. He's working from within to solve the problem and that gives him an edge over everybody else. I also like the fact that he goes about his business humanely, but I won't kid you, that's just a bonus. If I believed that we could sort out this mess by slicing you up in agonising, brutal ways, you wouldn't get any sympathy from me. I'd feel bad about it, but that wouldn't stop me forging ahead.'

'He says such nasty things sometimes, doesn't he?' Ciara tuts.

'He's no saint, that's for sure,' I mutter.

'Then again, this is hardly a time for saints, is it?' Reilly notes.

'True,' I nod. 'So how'd you find your way here? Did you follow the arrows?'

'No.' Reilly scratches the back of his neck. 'I was on my way out of the city. I wanted to join a compound in the countryside or head for one of the zombie-free islands and try to gain entry. Then I ran into a pack of Angels on a mission. I would have avoided them, except I recognised someone with them. I tracked the pack until he parted company with the zombies, then revealed myself and asked what he was up to. When he explained what was going on here, I decided I wanted to be part of it. I offered my services. They were accepted. So here I am.'

'Who was the guy you recognised?' I ask.

'You'll find out soon,' Reilly says. 'Dr Oystein returned earlier today and my contact was with him. I'm guessing the pair of them will want to see you.'

I get a prickle of excitement when I hear that the mysterious doctor is back. I was starting to think that I'd only dreamt about him. It seems like months since he introduced himself to me and took me on my first tour of the building.

'One last question. Do you know where Rage is?'

Reilly grimaces. 'We hauled him out of the Tube a couple of days ago. I've been watching my back since then.'

I bare my teeth in a vicious grin. 'I thought you trusted him.'

'I never said that,' Reilly corrects me. 'I said that Dr Oystein trusts him, and I trust Dr Oystein. I protected Rage because the doctor asked me to. That doesn't mean I liked it. And it doesn't mean I feel safe now that he's out on the prowl.'

Reilly looks around nervously and touches the handle of the stun gun which he has strapped to his side. 'Truth be told, I'm crapping myself.'

I laugh harshly. 'You should become one of us, Reilly. We don't crap, we just vomit.'

With that, I hop down and head back to the gym, treading carefully, judging the shadows as I pass, on the lookout for a cherubic monster.

SEVENTEEN

Now that Dr Oystein is back, I expect him to summon me for a meeting, but there's no sign of him that evening or night, and I head to bed at the usual time, surprised and frustrated.

When I mention the doctor's return to the others, they're not that bothered. Shane and Jakob say that they already knew. Ashtat and Carl didn't, but it's not a big deal for them, since they're accustomed to him coming and going.

'I never thought to tell you,' Shane shrugs when I

ask why he didn't let me know. 'It's not like we announce it with bugles every time he returns.'

In the morning I report for training again with Master Zhang. He lobs me around and slams me down hard on my back, time after time, studying the way I land, making suggestions, urging me to twist an arm this way, a leg that way.

After one particularly vicious slam dunk that makes me cry out loud, someone gasps theatrically and says, 'I hope that's as painful as it looks from here.'

I glance around, spirits rising, thinking it must be Dr Oystein, even though that would be a strange thing for him to say. But it's not the doctor. It's Rage, standing by the wall and smirking.

'Nice to see you again, Becky,' Rage says with fake sweetness. 'Last time I saw you, you were hanging naked in the Groove Tube.'

'Same here,' I sneer. 'Sorry for your little problem.'

'What do you mean?'

I cock the smallest finger on my right hand and flex it a couple of times.

Rage laughs. 'I don't worry about those sorts of

things any more. You'll have to do better than that to wind me up.'

'I'll do my best,' I snarl.

'Do you get the feeling she doesn't like me?' Rage asks Master Zhang.

'I have no interest in your petty squabbles,' Zhang says as I stand and grimace, still aching from when he threw me. 'In my company, you will treat one another with respect, as all of my students must.'

'You've been training Rage too?' I ask.

'For the last couple of days, yes,' Zhang nods.

'Be careful what you teach him,' I growl. 'He might use it against you.'

'Now, now, Becky,' Rage smiles. 'Remember what Master Zhang told you. It's all about *respect*.'

'Respect this,' I spit, giving him the finger.

'Enough,' Zhang says quietly. 'I will not tolerate disobedience.'

'Hear that?' Rage beams. 'You're gonna have a hard time –'

'That applies to you as well,' Zhang stops him. 'Both of you will be silent.'

I expect Rage to challenge Master Zhang, but he shuts up immediately and bows politely. I glare at him but hold my tongue.

'Oystein told me of your feud,' Zhang says, 'but that is not why I have kept you apart. I prefer to train new recruits by themselves for the first few days, so that I can evaluate them independently.'

'I bet I'm doing better than you,' Rage murmurs to me.

I ignore him, as does Master Zhang.

'There is a test that I subject my students to, usually after a couple of weeks,' Zhang continues. 'But Oystein wishes to speak with both of you later today, to explain more about our history and goals. I have decided to give you the test ahead of that meeting.'

'Why?' Rage asks.

'It is an important test,' Zhang says. 'If you fail, it will be an indication that you are not cut out for life as a fully active Angel. If Oystein knows that you will not be taking part in our more serious missions, it might affect what he chooses to share with you.'

'You mean, if we turn out to be a pair of losers, he won't want to waste too much time on us,' I grunt.

'Precisely,' Zhang says smoothly, then heads to the door and nods for us to follow him.

'You're not giving us the test here?' Rage asks as we turn into the corridor.

'No,' he says. 'We need reviveds for the test.' He looks back at us and his eyes glitter. '*Lots* of reviveds.'

Rage and I share a worried glance, then trail Master Zhang through the building. He stops off at a small storage room to pick up a couple of rucksacks, then leads us outside and over to Waterloo Station. We pass one of the speakers along the way, but he doesn't bother to turn it off.

'What's that noise?' Rage winces.

'I'll tell you about it sometime, if you pass this test,' I grin, delighted to know something he doesn't.

Zhang leads us up to the station concourse. This used to be one of the busiest train stations in London, but now it's home to hundreds of resting reviveds. The mindless zombies are scattered around the concourse, squatting, sitting, lying down, or just standing, waiting for night to fall. It's strange to think that so many of them are on our doorstep. I haven't seen any since I came to County Hall.

I stare at the old ticket machines, the shops and restaurants, trying to recall what it would have been like back in the day, wanting to feel nostalgic. But it's getting harder to remember what the world was like, to treat the memories as if they're real, rather than fragments of some crazy dream I once had.

'This is a very straightforward task,' Zhang says. He points towards the far end of the concourse, to an open doorway at the rear of the station. 'I want you to race to that exit. If you make it out in one piece, you pass the test.'

'That's all?' Rage frowns. 'But that's too easy. The zombies won't attack us. They know we're the same as them. Unless these are different to the ones I've seen elsewhere?'

'They are no different,' Zhang says. 'I did not arrange for them to be present, or interfere with them in any way. These are the usual residents, reviveds who have chosen to base themselves here.'

'Then what's the catch?' Rage asks.

'The rucksacks of course,' I tell him.

'Correct,' Zhang says. He passes one of the rucksacks

to me, the other to Rage, and gestures at us to put them on.

'I still don't get it,' Rage growls. 'They're not heavy. They won't slow us down.'

'They are not meant to slow you down,' Master Zhang tuts, then drives the fingers of his right hand into the rucksack on Rage's back, making five holes in it, before doing the same thing to mine.

The scent of fresh brains instantly fills the air and my lips tighten.

'This isn't good,' Rage mutters as the heads of the zombies closest to us start to lift.

'If you stood still, they would come and examine you,' Zhang says. 'When they realised that the brains are stored in your rucksacks, they'd let you be – revids do not fight with one another – and stand nearby, waiting, hoping to finish off any scraps that you might leave behind.'

'But we're not going to stand still, are we?' I sigh.

'No,' Zhang says. 'You are going to run.' He pokes some more holes in our rucksacks. '*Now.*'

Rage swears under his breath and shoots a dirty look

at Master Zhang. Then, since he has no other choice, he runs towards the zombies, who are stirring and getting to their feet. And since I have no choice either, I race after him, closing in quickly on the growing, undead wall of snarling, hungry reviveds.

EIGHTEEN

Rage barrels into several of the zombies, sending them flying. They howl with anger and excitement, more of them becoming alert, catching the scent of brains, closing in on us, fangs bared, finger bones twitching.

I take advantage of the confusion Rage has caused and angle to the right, hoping to slip by unnoticed. But other zombies who were sheltering on the platforms have heard the noises and come to investigate. When they spot me tearing by, they clamber over the ticket barriers and surge towards me in a mob, forcing me back into the centre of the concourse.

Rage is surrounded and is lashing out with his fists, trying to shove past those who block his way. It looks impossible, but he's kept up his momentum, like a burly rugby player forcing back a scrum.

I take a different approach. As zombies clutch at me and throw themselves in my path, I duck and shimmy and veer around them. I've been in a situation like this before, in Liverpool Street, when I was trying to escape with Sister Clare of the Shnax, so I put that experience to good use.

A sprawling zombie – he looks like he was a construction worker when he was alive – grabs my left leg just above my ankle and pulls me down. I kick out at him as I fall and he slides away from me. I realise he has no legs – they look like they were torn from him at the knees when he was turned – which is why he's lying on the floor.

Taking advantage of my unexpected fall, I slip through the legs of a couple of zombies ahead of me. One is a woman in a miniskirt. I grab hold of the skirt and spin her around, so that she clatters into several other zombies and knocks them over. As the skirt rips, I let her go, propel myself to my feet and carry on.

Rage has found a way through the press of zombies around him and has picked up speed. He calls cheerfully to me, 'This is the life, isn't it?'

I ignore him and stay focused on the reviveds, ducking their grasping fingers, kicking out at them, looking for open channels that I can exploit.

Master Zhang is trailing us, slowly, as if out for a Sunday stroll. He watches calmly, but not too curiously. I guess he's seen all this lots of times before.

A girl my own sort of age grabs the rucksack on my back and tries to wrestle it from me, either realising that the smell is coming from there, or simply seeing it as the best way to slow me down. I turn sharply and slam the flat of my palm up into her chin, snapping her head back and knocking her loose.

'An interesting move,' Master Zhang says. 'Most people in your position would have simply punched her.'

I don't reply. There's no time. Before the girl staggers away from me, I grab her and force her to her knees. Then I step on to her back and launch myself forward, flying over the heads of a pack of zombies who were closing in on me.

'Oh, now even I've got to applaud that one,' Rage booms, clapping loudly. He's been forced to a standstill close to where I land. 'How about we do this as a team?' he bellows, offering me his hand.

'Get stuffed,' I snap, and look for another small zombie that I can use as a springboard.

This time, as I'm hurling myself into the air, one of the reviveds catches hold of my left foot and hauls me to the floor. A cluster of them press in around me, fingers clawing at my face, trying to rip my head open, to get to the juicy brain which they think is the source of the smell.

'No!' I scream, pushing them back and struggling to my feet. I look around desperately, hoping that Master Zhang will help. But he just stands there, gazing at me, challenging me with his expression to figure my own way out of this mess.

Rage is moving forward again. He's snapped an arm off one of the zombies and is using it as a club, lashing out at anyone within range. Many of the zombies who get knocked back by him shake their heads, then refocus on me, figuring I offer easier pickings. A huge crowd of them starts to close in around me.

'Sod this,' I pant, knowing my number's up if I don't act swiftly.

Wriggling free of the rucksack, I rip it open and start throwing slivers of brain around, as if it was some weird kind of confetti. When the zombies spot the grey chunks, they go wild, but now they're concentrating on the bits of brain, trying to catch them as I toss them about, emptying the rucksack as quickly as I can.

When the rucksack is clean, I let it drop and fall still, letting the zombies see that I'm not trying to escape, that I have no need to run, that I'm the same as them.

A few of the reviveds sniff me suspiciously, growling like dogs, but then they leave me be and tear the remains of the rucksack to shreds, trying to squeeze out any last morsels of brain that might be hidden in the folds.

I look up at Master Zhang, shamefully, as the zombies part around me, but he's following Rage, no longer interested in me. I think about heading back to County Hall, or maybe just slipping away completely, figuring that's the end of my career as an Angel. But I want to see what happens to Rage. I'm hoping he'll brick it like I did and cast his rucksack aside.

But Rage is like a wrecking ball. The zombies slow him down, but they can't stop him. He slaps them back with the arm, punches and kicks them when the arm is no longer any good, sticks his head down and forces his way forward, refusing to accept defeat. I almost cheer on the rampaging brute, but then I recall how he killed Dr Cerveris and deserted the rest of the zom heads, and I hold my tongue.

He finally makes it to the end of the concourse and squeezes through the exit. As soon as he's out, he tears off the rucksack and lobs it back inside the station. The reviveds scurry after it, quickly losing interest in him, as they lost it in me.

'Now *that* was fun,' Rage grins as we join him outside. He wipes blood – not his own – from his face. 'I guess some of us have what it takes, Becky, and some of us don't.'

'Bite me,' I snarl, then cast a miserable look at Master Zhang. 'I guess this means I've had it.'

'Not at all,' he says, surprising both of us.

'What are you talking about?' Rage snaps. 'She failed.'

'No,' Zhang says. 'The test is designed to measure one's bravery, ingenuity and strength, but also one's level of common sense. Almost no novice Angel has made it all the way across the concourse. In fact you are only the third, and the other two made it with cunning and speed, not sheer muscle power.'

'Sweet!' Rage beams, thrilled with himself.

'So . . . I didn't fail?' I frown.

'No. You showed that you were willing to face adversity, and you handled yourself well. In fact you made it further than most. But just as importantly, when you realised you could go no further, you were sensible enough to rid yourself of the beacon which was attracting the reviveds. Those who fail are those who break too early with fear, or those who lack the wit to throw away the rucksack.'

'Then I did better than Rage, in a way,' I joke.

'In your dreams,' Rage grunts.

'There is no better or worse in my eyes,' Master Zhang says. 'You both passed. That is the end of the matter.'

With that, he heads back to County Hall, but circles round the rear of the station this time, rather than return through the concourse. Rage slides up beside me as we trail our mentor. He points to himself and says, 'One of three.' Then he points to me and says, 'One of *who cares?*'

He laughs and moves on before I can reply, leaving me to scowl angrily at his back with a mixture of hatred, jealousy and grudging respect.

NINETEEN

Master Zhang leads Rage and me back to the room in County Hall where I was training earlier. He says that since he has both of us with him, he will train with the pair of us for the rest of the session.

I get excited when I hear that. After passing our Waterloo-based test, I assume that we're ready to move on, that he'll start teaching us complicated moves. But it's business as usual, the only change being that he now takes turns to throw us to the floor. I'm pleased to see that Rage is treated the same way I am, but disappointed that Master Zhang isn't taking us a few stages further forward.

We've been back about an hour when the door opens and Dr Oystein steps into the room. He's not alone. Ashtat, Carl, Shane and Jakob are with him, as well as a man I recognise but didn't expect to see here.

'Mr Burke?' I gasp.

'Hello again, B,' my ex-teacher says, as our training draws to a halt. 'We seem to keep meeting in the strangest of places, don't we?'

As I gawp at my old teacher, I recall what Reilly said about seeing someone he knew with a pack of Angels after he'd deserted the army following the riots in the underground complex, and it starts to make sense.

Billy Burke had worked in the complex with Reilly, but he'd never seemed to fit in with the soldiers and scientists. Of them all, only he truly cared about the welfare of the zom heads. That was why they'd recruited him, to help them with the sometimes rebellious teenagers.

I should have figured this out before. Having severed his ties with the army, Reilly wouldn't have wanted to approach any of his old crew. Burke was different. Reilly wouldn't have considered him the same as the

others. He'd have felt he could trust the compassionate counsellor.

'Josh told me he'd released you,' Burke says as I stand, staring at him silently. 'I was hoping you'd find your way here. That's why I passed on your description to Dr Oystein.'

I frown. '*You* told the doc about me?'

'Yes,' Dr Oystein answers. 'That is how I knew your name when you first came here, and some of your background.'

I scratch my ear. 'I thought Reilly spotted me on the cameras and told you.'

The doctor shakes his head. 'No. It was Billy.'

'Well . . . thanks . . . I guess,' I mutter, lowering my hand.

'It is good to see you again, B,' Dr Oystein says. 'You have settled in nicely, I hear.'

'I'm doing all right,' I sniff.

'Zhang,' Dr Oystein says, bowing towards our mentor.

Master Zhang bows in return.

'How did our pair of fledgling Angels fare with their test earlier?' Dr Oystein asks.

'They passed,' Zhang says simply, giving us no more credit than that.

'I told you they would,' Burke smiles. 'They're a rare pair, those two.'

'Some of us are rarer than others,' Rage says, cocking an eyebrow at me.

'Why don't you shut up for once?' I snarl.

'Who's gonna make me?' Rage growls, squaring up to me.

'I would rather you did not fight,' Dr Oystein says quietly, and Rage immediately goes all sheepish and shuffles his feet.

'Sorry,' he mutters.

'Oh, isn't he a good boy,' I coo, then spit with contempt, which isn't easy with my dry mouth. 'Don't trust him, Dr Oystein. He's only buttering you up to make you like him, the same way he did with Dr Cerveris.'

'Why should I?' Rage counters. 'Dr Oystein hasn't tried to cage me up like those other buggers did. I'm free to leave whenever I please.'

'And you will,' I snort. 'When it suits you. And you'll

probably kill a few of us along the way, just for the hell of it.'

Rage shrugs and turns to Dr Oystein. 'I told you, when I saw her in the lab, that she'd have nothing good to say about me.'

'Yes, you did,' the doctor nods. 'And B has warned us to be wary of you. I have chosen to ignore both of your opinions, so please save your bickering for another time. You are going to be room-mates, so you will have plenty of –'

'You're not sticking him in with us!' I shout.

'Please, B, there is no need to raise your voice.'

'But –'

'Please,' Dr Oystein says again. The fact that he sounds as if he is actually asking, rather than issuing an order, slows me in my tracks. I grumble something beneath my breath but otherwise hold my tongue.

Carl and the others are watching our exchange with interest, eyeing up Rage.

'This is Michael Jarman,' Dr Oystein says to them. 'But he prefers –'

'*Michael Jarman?*' I laugh.

'You didn't think I was christened Rage, did you?' he says.

'I brought you here to meet him, because Rage will be sharing your room if nobody has any objections,' Dr Oystein continues, then smiles fleetingly at me. 'With the noted exception of Miss Smith.'

'If he moves in, I'm moving out,' I say stiffly.

Dr Oystein sighs. 'That would be regrettable. I let everyone decide where they want to room once they have adjusted to life here, but I prefer to assign places to begin with. If you choose not to respect my decision, I will take that as a sign that you do not trust my judgement.'

'No, it's not that . . . I mean I don't . . .' I growl with frustration. 'He's a killer. He betrayed me and the other zom heads.'

'I know.'

'But you want to stick him in with me anyway?'

'Yes.'

Dr Oystein's expression never alters.

'Fine,' I grunt. 'Whatever.'

'Thank you,' he says and seeks the approval of the

others. They shrug, knowing nothing about Rage or my beef with him. 'In that case, thank you for your time, and feel free to return to your usual duties. B and Rage, would you please accompany Mr Burke and myself on a short walk? There are certain matters I wish to discuss with the pair of you.'

'Sure,' I say, shooting Rage an evil look. He only smirks in return.

We file out, Dr Oystein and Burke in front, Rage and me a few steps behind, keeping as far apart from one another as we can.

TWENTY

We wind our way through the corridors of County Hall, Dr Oystein taking his time. Burke looks back at me. 'I was so relieved when Josh said that he'd spared you.'

'Yeah, well, I was the only one he did spare,' I say bitterly, recalling how he torched the other zom heads.

Burke looks contrite. 'If I'd been there, I would have tried to stop him.'

'Really?' I challenge him. 'You seemed to be fine with what he was doing the rest of the time.'

My old teacher sighs heavily. 'I'm sorry for all of the

deception and lies. They thought I was on their side. They knew I didn't approve of everything they were doing, but they had no idea I was in league with Dr Oystein. I had to play ball or they might have become suspicious.'

'You were a spy?' I frown.

'Yes.'

'I do not trust the military,' Dr Oystein says without pausing or turning. 'They wish to restore order to the world, which is my wish too, but they want to do so on their own terms. We must be wary of them. They include me in some of their plans and experiments, since they respect my specialist knowledge of the undead, but I like to keep track of all that I am excluded from too. Billy agreed to act as my inside man, as he had already earned their trust before our paths crossed.'

'You mean you were working for the army before you met Dr Oystein?'

Burke nods.

'Not especially loyal, are you?' I snort.

'I'm loyal to those I deem deserving of loyalty,' he says sharply.

Silence falls again. We exit the building on to the riverbank. I think for a second that Dr Oystein plans to take us bowling, but then I see that he's heading for the aquarium. 'Was the story about you convincing Josh and the others to feed me and keep me revitalised the truth?' I ask Burke.

'Yes,' he says.

'Thanks,' I mutter.

'No need. You would have done the same for me.' I raise an eyebrow and Burke chuckles wryly. 'Well, I like to tell myself that you would.'

We share a quick grin, then we're stepping off the path into the dim, silent world of the aquarium. I came here in the past, but not since I rocked up at County Hall as a zombie. I hadn't even thought about this place. Fish have been among the last things on my mind recently.

I find, to my surprise, that most of the tanks are still in working order, teeming with underwater life as they were before.

'Do zombies eat fish brains?' I ask.

'Only those of a certain size,' Dr Oystein says. 'We

thrive primarily on human brains, but those of larger animals and fish are nourishing too. Fortunately a small band of people managed to drive back the zombies on the day of the attack and barricade themselves in here. Ciara was one of them. They survived and hung on until we set up camp in County Hall. All except Ciara chose to be relocated to compounds beyond the city once we gave them that option. She had grown fond of the place, and of my Angels, so she decided to stay.'

We move in silence from one tank to another, studying an array of fish, turtles, squid and all sorts of weird species. Many are beautifully coloured and strangely shaped, and I'm reminded of how exotic this place seemed when I came here as a child. I never saw the appeal of aquariums before I visited. I thought they were dull places for nerds who loved goldfish.

We come to a glass tunnel through a huge tank of sharks. There are other things in there with them, but who takes notice of anything else when you spot a shark?

Dr Oystein draws to a halt in the middle of the tunnel and gazes around. 'I did not know much about

the maintenance of aquariums when I first moved in, but I have made it my business to learn. Some of my Angels share my passion and tend to the tanks in my absence. Perhaps one of you will wish to help too.'

Rage shakes his head. 'I only like fish when it's in batter and served up with chips.'

'Philistine,' I sneer.

'Up yours,' he says. 'They don't do anything for me. I'd rather go on safari than deep-sea diving.'

'I doubt if anyone will be going on safari any time in the near future,' Dr Oystein murmurs. 'And the zoos have been picked clean of their stock by now — I sent teams to check, in case we could harvest more brains. But at least this small part of our natural heritage survives.'

Dr Oystein sits down and nods for us to join him on the floor. He says nothing for a moment, relishing the underwater world which we've become a temporary part of. Then he makes a happy sighing sound.

'For many decades I have found God in the creatures of the sea,' he says. 'The sheer diversity of life, the crazy shapes and colours, the way they can adapt and flour- ish . . . I defy anyone to stroll through an aquarium and tell me our world could throw forth such wonders without the guiding hand of a higher power.'

'You're not a fan of Darwin then?' Rage snickers.

'Oh, I believe in evolution,' Dr Oystein says. 'But you do not have to exclude one at the expense of the other. All creatures – ourselves included – are servants of nature and the changing forces of the world in which we live. But how can such a world have come into being by accident? If evolution was the only force at work, large, dull, powerful beasts would have prevailed and stamped their mark on this planet long ago. Only a curious, playful God would have populated our shores and seas with such a glittering, spellbinding array of specimens.'

Dr Oystein turns his gaze away from the sharks to look us in the eye, one after the other, as he speaks.

'I did not bring you here by chance. As I said, I find God in places like this, and God is what I wish to discuss. I was not always a believer, so I will not be dismayed if you do not share my beliefs. I am not looking to convert either of you, merely to explain how and why I came to put together my team of Angels.

'I was born shortly after the turn of the twentieth century. It might seem odd, but I no longer recall the exact date. It is even possible that I was born in the late nineteenth century, though I do not think I am quite that old.

'For the first thirty-five or forty years of my life, I was an atheist. I hurled the works of Darwin and other scientists at those who clung to the ways of what I thought was a ridiculous, outdated past. Then, in the 1930s, in the lead-up to the Second World War, God found me and I realised what a fool I had been.' Dr Oystein lowers his gaze and sighs again, sadly this time.

'God found me,' he repeats in a cracked voice, 'but not before the Nazis found me first . . .'

TWENTY
-ONE

Dr Oystein travelled around Europe with his parents when he was a child. As a man, he continued to tour the world, but ended up settling in Poland, where his wife was from and where his elder brother – also a doctor – had set up home.

They were happy years, he tells us, the brothers working together, raising their families, enjoying the lull between the wars. Dr Oystein and his brother were noted geneticists who could have lived anywhere – they had offers from across the globe – but they were happy in Poland.

Then the Nazis invaded. Dr Oystein's instincts told him to flee, but his wife and children didn't want to leave their home and his brother refused to go too. With an uneasy feeling, he agreed to remain and hoped that he would be allowed to carry on his work in peace and quiet, since he had no strong political ties and wasn't a member of any of the religions or races which the Nazis despised.

Unfortunately for the doctor, the Nazis were almost as interested in genetics as they were in killing Jews and gypsies. They were intent on improving the human form and creating a master race. They saw Dr Oystein and his brother as key allies in their quest to overcome the weaknesses of nature.

When Dr Oystein rejected their advances, he was imprisoned in a concentration camp along with his brother and their families. The camps weren't as hellish as the death camps which were built later in the war, but the chances of survival were slim all the same.

'If the guards disliked you,' Dr Oystein says quietly, 'they worked you until you could work no more, then executed you for failing to complete your tasks. Or they tortured you until you confessed to whatever crime they wished to charge you with. They might make you stand still for hours on end, under the threat of death if you moved, then shoot you when you collapsed from sheer exhaustion.'

Dr Oystein had three children. His brother had four. The Nazis killed one of Dr Oystein's children and two of his brother's, and made it clear that their wives and the surviving children would be executed as well if the brothers didn't do as they were told. When they saw what they were up against, they agreed to be shipped off to a secret unit to work for their monstrous new masters.

The Nazis yearned to unravel the secrets of life and death, to bring the dead back from beyond the grave. There were two reasons. One was to create an army of undead soldiers, to give them an advantage in the war. The other was so that they could survive forever, to indefinitely enjoy the pleasures of the new society which they were hell-bent on creating.

Dr Oystein and his brother were part of an elite team, some of the greatest minds in the world, all working towards the same warped goal. Some were there by force, some by choice. It didn't matter. They all had to slave away as hard as they could. Nazis were not known for their tolerance of failure.

'We made huge strides forward,' Dr Oystein says without any hint of pride. 'We unlocked secrets which are still beyond the knowledge of geneticists today. If we had been allowed to share our findings with the world, we would have been hailed as wonders and people of your generation would be benefiting from our discoveries. But the Nazis were selfish. Records of our advances were buried away in mounds of paperwork, far from prying eyes.'

Dr Oystein created the first revived. He brought a woman back to life after she had died of malnutrition in a concentration camp. (He says that most of their cadavers were drawn from the camps.)

'It should have been a wondrous moment,' he whispers. 'I had done what only God had previously achieved. Mankind's potential skyrocketed. The future opened up to us as it never had before. Immortality – or at least a vastly extended life – became ours for the taking.'

But instead he felt wretched, partly because he knew the Nazis would take his discovery and do terrible things with it, but also because he felt that he had broken the laws of the universe, and he was sure that nothing good could come of that.

The Nazis rejoiced. The revived was a mindless, howling, savage beast, of no practical use to them, but they were confident that the doctor and his team would build on this breakthrough and find a way to restore the mind as well as the body. But they couldn't. No matter how many corpses they brought back to life, they couldn't get the brains to work. Every zombie was a drooling, senseless wreck.

'The Nazis discussed dropping the living dead behind enemy lines,' Dr Oystein says, 'but as vicious as they were, they were not fools. They knew they could not manage the spread of the reviveds once they released them, and they had no wish to inherit a world of deadly, infectious zombies.'

Dr Oystein was sure that they had pushed the project as far as they could. He didn't share that view with the Nazis, but all of his results suggested to him that they had come to a dead end. He didn't think the brain of a corpse could ever be restored.

While all this was happening, the Nazis kept presenting the brothers with regular reports of their wives and children, photographs and letters to prove that they were alive and well. One day that stopped. They were told that the information was being withheld until they created a revitalised specimen, but the doctors were afraid that something terrible had happened.

'And we were right,' Dr Oystein mutters. 'I found out much later that both of my remaining children had died. My wife went wild and attacked those who had imprisoned her. My brother's wife tried to pull her away, to calm her down.

'The women were shot by an over-eager guard. That left only my brother's daughter and son. The girl died a couple of years later, but the boy survived.' Dr Oystein coughs and looks away. 'I thought of my nephew often over the decades but never sought him out. I didn't want him to see what I had become.'

With no news of their loved ones, and fearing the worst, the brothers made up their minds to escape.

They hated working for the Nazis, and if their families had been executed, they had nothing to lose — their own lives didn't matter to them. They put a lot of time and thought into their plan, and almost pulled it off. But their laboratory was one of the most highly guarded prisons in the world. Luck went against them on the night of their escape. They were caught and tortured.

Under interrogation, Dr Oystein told the Nazis that he thought it was impossible to revitalise a subject, that the vacant zombies in their holding cells were as good as it was ever going to get. The Nazis were furious. They decided to teach the brothers a vicious lesson, to serve as an example. They infected the pair with the undead gene and turned them into zombies.

'That should have been the end of us,' Dr Oystein says, eyes distant as he remembers that dark, long-ago day. 'But there was something nobody had counted on. Like every other revived, I could not be brought back to consciousness by the hand of man. But there was another at work, a doctor of sorts, whose power was far greater than mine or anyone else's.

TWENTY -TWO

Dr Oystein pauses to study the sharks. I glance around at the others, disturbed by what I've been told. Burke returns my gaze calmly, giving no sign whether he buys this or not. Rage is more direct. He puts a finger to the side of his head and twirls it around — *cuckoo!* But I can tell by the way he peeks guiltily at Dr Oystein as he lowers his arm that the story has troubled him too.

'God spoke to me when He saved me,' Dr Oystein continues. 'He told me what had happened, why I had been spared, what I must do.'

The reviveds were kept in holding pens, secure but

not foolproof. Plenty of security measures were in place, but all had been designed with the limitations of brainless subjects in mind. The Nazis hadn't considered the threat of a conscious, intelligent zombie.

Dr Oystein freed the reviveds and set them on the soldiers and scientists, who were taken by surprise. Nobody was spared. The zombies ran riot, killing or converting everyone, helped by the doctor, who opened doors and sought out hiding places.

When all of the humans had been disposed of, Dr Oystein destroyed every last scrap of paperwork and evidence of what had been going on. He knew that reports had been sent to officials elsewhere, but he did what he could to limit the damage. After that, with a heavy heart, he killed all of the zombies one by one, ripping out their brains to ensure they were never brought back to life again.

Dr Oystein doesn't mention his brother, but I'm sure he must have killed him too. I'm not surprised that he doesn't go into specifics. It's not the sort of thing I imagine you want to spend a lot of time thinking about.

His work finished, Dr Oystein slipped away into the

night, to set about the mission which he had been given by the voice inside his head.

God told Dr Oystein that the human race had become too violent and destructive. Bringing the dead back to life was the final straw. There had to be a reckoning, like when the Bible said that He flooded the world. A thinning of the ranks. A cleansing.

The voice told Dr Oystein that there would be a plague of zombies in the near future. On a day of divine destiny, a war would break out between mankind and the living dead.

'Are you saying God unleashed the zombies?' I ask incredulously, unable to keep quiet any longer.

'Of course not,' Dr Oystein replies. 'But God saw that scientists would conduct fresh experiments and create new strains of the zombie gene. And one day one of them would accidentally or deliberately release an airborne strain which would sweep the globe and convert millions of humans into undead monsters. He could have spared us the agony if He had wished, but honestly, B, can you think of any good reason why He should have intervened?'

'Lots of innocent people died,' I mutter.

Dr Oystein nods. 'They always do. That is the nature of our world. But do you think it was a perfect society, that our leaders were just and good, that as a race we were not guilty of unimaginable, unpardonable crimes?'

'You can't punish everyone for the sins of a few,' Rage growls.

'Of course you can,' Dr Oystein says. 'Just step outside and look around if you do not believe that. As a people, we offended our creator and turned on our own like jackals. We soiled this world. Was the plague of zombies a harsh judgement? Perhaps. But unfair? I think not.'

Dr Oystein shakes his head when nobody says anything else, then continues.

He criss-crossed the world in the years to come, building up contacts among all sorts of officials. His first priority was to crack down on undead outbreaks, and to contain them when they happened. With the help of his contacts, he kept the existence of zombies a secret. Rumours trickled out every so often, but nobody in their right mind paid any attention to them. Hollywood film makers were paid to weave wild tales about the living dead, to turn them into movie monsters, like Dracula or the Mummy.

But no matter how hard he worked, the experiments continued. Nazi scientists in hiding created their own small zombie armies in the hope of launching a bid to control the world again. Some sold their secrets to rich men or leaders in countries where power struggles were a way of life.

Dr Oystein experimented too. God had told him that he would need to fight fire with fire if he was to have any chance of redeeming the human race. The doctor was the first of what could be a highly effective force of revitaliseds. If he could find a way to restore others, the world might regain a sliver of hope.

'Although it repulsed me, I returned to my work,' he says, hanging his head with shame. 'If there was any other way, I would have seized it gladly, but there wasn't.'

'What makes you think you're any better than the rest of the creeps then?' I sneer. 'Maybe the airborne gene was created by one of *your* associates, using technology that *you* pioneered.'

'Perhaps,' Dr Oystein nods. 'But I do not think that is the case. I have learnt much about the gene over the decades, but the airborne strain was new to me. It is a destructive strain, while my work has been focused on the positive possibilities, on the human mind and its restoration.

'I finally figured out a way to create revitaliseds,' he goes on. 'I hoped to perfect a vaccine that would stop people returning to life when they were infected — if zombies could only kill, not convert, they would be far easier to deal with. Failing that, I hoped to provide the undead with the ability to recover their wits, so that they could be reasoned with.

'Until that point I had experimented solely on corpses or on those who had been revived. But if prevention was to serve as the key to our survival, it meant I would have to –'

'– experiment on living people,' Rage cuts in, beating Dr Oystein to the punch. He doesn't look outraged, simply fascinated.

'You're sick,' I snarl, but for once I'm not insulting Rage. My comment is directed at Dr Oystein. I rise and glare at him. 'You're just like the Nazis and the scientists who were experimenting on the zom heads.'

'I do not claim to be any nobler than them,' Dr Oystein says softly. 'I have done many dreadful things and you have every right to vilify me.'

'Then why shouldn't I?' I snap. 'You said I was an Angel. You offered protection and told me we could do good. Why should I accept the word of a man who experimented on living people and probably killed more than a few in the process?'

'Many have died at my hands over the years,' he admits. 'I see their faces every night, even though I don't dream.'

'So why should I pledge myself to you?' I press. 'Why shouldn't I storm out of here and never look back?'

Dr Oystein shrugs. 'Because I was successful,' he whispers. 'I found a way to revitalise zombies.'

Now it's my turn to shrug. 'So? Does that mean we should forgive you?'

Dr Oystein looks up at last. There's no anger in his gaze, only misery. 'I am not worthy of forgiveness, but I do think that I am worthy of your support.'

'Why?' I ask again, barking the question this time.

'Because I created you,' Dr Oystein says. And as I stare at him, trying to figure out what he means, he says, 'Tell me, B, do you have a little c-shaped scar on your upper right thigh?'

In the silence that follows, all I can do is stare at him, then through the glass walls of the tunnel at the sharks circling patiently, their wide mouths lifting at the corners, almost in wicked, mocking smiles.

TWENTY -THREE

I've had the c-shaped scar since I was two or three years old. I was injected with an experimental flu vaccine. It worked a treat and I've never had so much as a sniffle since. I sometimes thought it was odd that the vaccine hadn't taken off — nobody else I knew had been vaccinated with it. I figured there must have been side effects which I'd been lucky enough to avoid.

'Haven't you wondered why virtually all of the revitaliseds are teenagers?' Burke asks softly.

I stare at him, thinking back. In the underground complex I never saw any adult revitaliseds. I assumed they were being held in a different section, that we'd been grouped together by age.

Apart from Dr Oystein and Master Zhang, they're all teenagers or younger here in County Hall too. Dr Oystein told me that adult revitaliseds were rare, but I never pushed it any further than that. I've got so used to being around others my own age that it didn't seem strange.

'I developed the vaccine about forty years ago,' Dr Oystein says. 'It is unpredictable and does not work in everyone. Many who have been vaccinated do not recover their senses when infected. Those who revitalise do so at different rates. The fastest has been eighteen hours. At six months, you are one of the slowest.'

'See?' Rage smiles. 'You're slow. It's official.'

I ignore him and stay focused on Dr Oystein.

'My intention was to have teams vaccinate every living person before the wave of reviveds broke across the world. But the vaccine was unstable. It could not be held in check indefinitely. If a person was not bitten by a zombie, after fifteen or so years it turned on its host. The body broke down. The bones and flesh liquefied.

It was swift – from start to finish, no more than half a day – and incredibly painful.'

'You're telling me that if I hadn't been attacked by zombies, I'd have ended up as a puddle of goo in another year or two?' I gasp.

The doctor nods and I laugh bitterly.

'You're some piece of work, doc. The Nazis had nothing on you.'

He flinches at the insult.

'But now that we've been infected . . .' Rage says.

'The vaccine will not harm us while it is fighting with the zombie gene,' Dr Oystein says. 'We are safe now that we have revitalised.

'If I had known when the day of reckoning was due, I could have vaccinated as many people as possible,' he continues. 'But God never revealed the date to me. If I had miscalculated, I could have wiped out the entire race by myself, no zombies required.'

Rage whistles softly. 'That's some crazy power. Were you ever tempted to . . . you know . . . just for the hell of it?'

We all stare at him.

'Come on,' he protests. 'You guys were thinking the same thing. If you had the world in the palm of your hand, and all you had to do was squeeze . . .'

'You're a sick, twisted bastard,' I sneer.

'No,' Dr Oystein says. 'Rage is right. I *was* tempted. But not in the way he thinks. I had no interest in crushing nations. I was tempted because I was afraid. I knew the terrors and hardships we must face, and I did not want to embrace such a future. It would have been easier to condemn mankind to a swift, certain end, to accept defeat and ensure that nobody need suffer the agonies of a long, drawn-out war of nightmarish proportions. Death by vaccine would have been simpler, the coward's way out.

'I am various low, despicable things,' Dr Oystein whispers, 'but I do not think I am a coward. I am guilty of many foul crimes, but I have always accepted my responsibilities. I ignored the pleas of my weaker self and remained true to my calling. If mankind is to perish, it will not be because I was found wanting.'

Dr Oystein rises and starts walking. The rest of us head after him. He moves faster than before, striding through the aquarium, leading us out into the open. On the riverbank he hurries to the wall overlooking the Thames and bends over it as if about to throw up.

'I'm sorry,' he moans, but it's unclear whether he's apologising to us or the souls of the people he experimented on and killed over the course of his long and dreadful life.

TWENTY
-FOUR

Dr Oystein stays facing the river for a couple of minutes while the rest of us stand back, waiting for him to recover.

'This guy needs to see a shrink,' Rage murmurs.

I turn to rip into him for being an insensitive pig, but I see by his expression that he wasn't having a dig. The big, ugly lump looks about as pitying as he ever could.

'I doubt if any ordinary professional could help him,' Burke says softly. 'This isn't a normal complaint. To have endured all that he has . . . I'm stunned he's not a gibbering wreck.'

'Do you believe everything he told us?' I ask. 'About Nazis, God, all that ...' I was about to say *crap* but decide that's not the right word, ' ... stuff?'

'We'll discuss that later,' Burke says and nods at Dr Oystein, who is turning from the river at last. He looks embarrassed.

'My apologies. Sometimes the guilt overwhelms me. I know that I have done what was asked of me, but there are days when that does not seem like a justifiable excuse. God did not authorise the experiments, the tests that went awry, the lives which I have sacrificed. I see no other way that I could have proceeded, but still I wonder ... and fear.'

He sighs and glances up at the London Eye, turning as smoothly as ever, the pods shining brightly against the backdrop of the cloudy sky.

'So why are all of your Angels teenagers?' I ask, to draw him back to what he was talking about earlier. 'Why didn't you vaccinate adults too?'

'I felt that children would be more appropriate,' Dr Oystein says. 'They are, generally speaking, more inno-cent and pure of heart than adults.'

'You wouldn't think like that if you'd gone to my school,' I mutter, and share a grin with Mr Burke.

Dr Oystein smiles ruefully. 'That was not the only factor. There were practical reasons too. Children were easier to vaccinate than adults — they received so many jabs that nobody took notice of one more. And since their bodies were undergoing natural changes during growth, they were better equipped to contain the vaccine — children generally held out a few years longer than grown-ups before succumbing to the side effects.

'Also, I distrusted adults. They were set in their ways, less open to fresh ideas and change. I needed soldiers who would think nothing of their own lives, who would dedicate themselves entirely to the cause. I decided that children were more likely to answer such a demanding call.

'Every year my team vaccinated a selection from newborns to teenagers in cities, towns and villages across the world. Every time I looked at the files – and I made a point of acknowledging each and every subject – I suffered a conflict of interests. I found myself hoping that the plague would strike soon, to spare the vaccinated children the painful death they would have to endure if it did not, yet also wishing that it wouldn't, because that would mean so many more people dying.'

Dr Oystein falls silent again, remembering some of the faces of the damned.

'How many did you vaccinate each year?' I ask.

'Several thousand,' he says. 'Always in a different area, with a fresh team under a different guise, to avert people's suspicions.'

'What do you mean?' Rage frowns.

'One year we offered a cure for the flu,' Dr Oystein explains. 'The next year we promoted a measles vaccine. The year after something to help prevent AIDS. Each time we hid behind a fake company or charity.'

'So if you've been doing this for decades . . .' I try to do the maths.

'Hundreds of thousands,' Dr Oystein says softly.

'How the hell do you cover up that many deaths?' I explode. 'Especially if they melted down into muck. I never read about anything like that in the Sunday papers.'

'As I already explained, I had contacts in high places,'

Dr Oystein says. 'They clamped down on any talk that might have compromised our position.'

'Still,' I mutter, '*somebody* must have leaked word of what was going on.'

'They did,' Burke says. 'It was all over the place, in self-published books and on the internet. I remember coming across articles back when I knew nothing about Dr Oystein or his work. Like any sane person, I dismissed them. Who could believe stories of a drug that made people melt?'

'Truth is stranger than fiction,' Rage says smugly, as if he's just come out with an incredibly original, witty line.

'All right,' I mutter. 'I'm getting it. You vaccinated thousands of kids every year to create an army of revitaliseds when the Apocalypse hit. So there must be, what, a few hundred thousand of us, ranging in age from adults down to babies?'

'Less,' Dr Oystein says. 'Many failed to revitalise, particularly those who had matured. Others were slaughtered during the assaults and their brains were eaten. Young children who revitalised either failed to follow the signs to my safe houses or reverted due to not being able to feed.

'We cannot be sure, but we think there are maybe a couple of thousand Angels worldwide, possibly less.'

'You didn't get a great return for all those sacrifices, did you, doc?' Rage asks quietly.

'No,' the doctor says, even quieter.

'And are there centres like this in different countries, full of Angels?' I ask.

'Yes,' Dr Oystein says hesitantly.

'Something wrong with the others?' I press.

'No. But they are not as important as the Angels in London.'

I laugh shortly. 'I bet your people say that to all the Angels.'

He shakes his head. 'We are in a unique position. Several of the revitaliseds who came to us here asked to be relocated once I revealed what I am about to reveal to you.'

'That sounds ominous,' Rage growls but his face is alight with curiosity. I bet mine is too. I haven't a clue what's coming next or how it can be any worse than what he's told us already.

'This is a universe of good and evil,' Dr Oystein says. 'I am sure you know from your lessons in school that for every action there is an equal and opposite reaction.'

'Quit with the dramatic build-up, doc,' Rage huffs. 'Give it to us straight.'

'Very well,' the doctor says as a rare angry spark flashes across his eyes. 'Just as there is an ultimate force of good in this universe, there is also one of evil. To put it into the terms I find easiest to understand, God is real but so is Satan.'

Rage's smirk fades. I get a sick feeling in my stomach. Burke looks away.

'When God revitalised me, it was an act of love,' Dr Oystein says. 'He did it because He wished to hand mankind a lifeline. He was obliged to punish us, but He wanted to give us a fighting chance in the war to come.

'If God had left me to my own devices, I would have remained a mindless revived. Other scientists would have continued their experiments and the airborne strain of the disease would have been developed. When the ferocious undead arose, humanity would have lacked champions. The living need us. We can go where they can't, fight in ways they cannot.

'But there are laws which even God abides by. They are laws of His making, but if He ignores them, what use are they? A law which does not apply to all is no real sort of law.

'The forces of good and evil do not engage one another directly,' Dr Oystein continues. 'Their followers clash all the time, humanity forever swaying between the extremes of right and wrong, taking a positive step forward here, a negative step backward there. But God told me that if He or Satan ever takes a direct role in the affairs of man – if they interfere in any way – then the other has the right to counteract that.'

'Tit for tat,' I whisper and Dr Oystein nods sombrely.

'That is why God so rarely reaches out to us. He might often wish to, when He looks down and sees us in pain, but He does not dare, because if He extends a hand of love, Satan can stretch forth a claw of hate.'

'This is bullshit,' I croak. 'It's madness.' I seek out Burke's gaze. 'Isn't it?' I shout.

Burke only shrugs uncomfortably.

'When God restored my consciousness,' Dr Oystein says, raising his voice ever so slightly, 'it allowed Satan to create his own mockery of the human form, a being of pure viciousness and spite who could wreak as much damage as I had the power to repair.

'I have sought long and hard for my demonic counterpart over the decades, but our paths never crossed. There were many occasions when I came close – and when he came close to tracking me down and striking at me, for he loathes me as much as I fear him – but something always kept us apart. Until now.'

Dr Oystein crosses his arms and trains his sights on me. 'You know evil's true name, don't you, B?'

'Get stuffed,' I whimper.

'Don't deny the truth. I can see the awareness in your eyes. Say it and spare me the unpleasant task. Please.'

'What the hell is he –' Rage starts to ask, but I blurt out the answer before he can finish.

'*Mr Dowling!*' I shout.

'Yes,' Dr Oystein says, shuddering. 'The clown with the smile of death. The creator of mutants and executioner of innocents. A creature of immense power and darkness, who relishes chaos and devastation, just like his grim master.

'Mr Dowling is the earthly representative of the force of ultimate evil. With the sinister clown's malevolent help, the Devil, as I call him, hopes to lead the zombies to victory and plunge our world into eternal, tormented night.

'The war between the living and the dead rages across the globe, but this is where it will be decided. London has been chosen as the key battleground. I set up base here for reasons I cannot define, and Mr Dowling has done likewise. The war we wage in this city of the damned will be the most instrumental of the conflict.

'We must take the fight to Mr Dowling,' Dr Oystein says, and his face betrays the terror he feels. 'He is our most direct and deadly nemesis. We will engage in a brutal, bloody battle to the death. If we triumph, peace and justice will reign and mankind can resume its quest to win heavenly favour.

'If we lose,' he concludes, and he doesn't need to drop his voice to make his sickening, dizzying point, 'every single one of us is damned and this world will become an outpost of Hell.'

To be continued . . .